The Girl from Uganda

Tengio Urrio

Spear Books Series

Sugar Daddy's Lover. *Rosemarie Owino*
Lover in the Sky. *Sam Kahiga*
Mystery Smugglers. *Mwangi Ruheni*
A Girl Cannot Go on Laughing all the time. *Magaga Alot*
The Love Root. *Mwangi Ruheni*
The Ivory Merchant. *Mwangi Gicheru*
A Brief Assignment. *Ayub Ndii*
A Taste of Business. *Aubrey Kalitera*
No Strings Attached. *Yusuf K. Dawood*
Queen of Gems. *Laban Erapu*
A Prisoner's Letter. *Aubrey Kalitera*
A Woman Reborn. *Koigi wa Wamwere*
The Bhang Syndicate. *Frank Saisi*
My Life in Crime. *John Kiriamiti*
Black Gold of Chepkube. *Wamugunda Geteria*
Ben Kamba 009 in Operation DXT. *David Maillu*
Son of Woman in Mombasa. *Charles Mangua*
The Ayah. *David Maillu*
A Worm in the Head. *Charles Githae*
Life and Times of a Bank Robber. *John Kiggia*
Twilight Woman. *Thomas Akare*
Son of Woman. *Charles Mangua*
A Tail in the Mouth. *Charles Mangua*
My Life with a Criminal: Milly's Story. *John Kiriamiti*
The Operator. *Chris Mwangi*
Birds of Kamiti. *Benjamin Bunde*
Nice People. *Wamugunda Geteria*
Times Beyond. *Omondi Mak'Oloo*
Mayor in Prison. *Karuga Wandai*
Lady in Chains. *Genga-Idowu*
Prison is Not a Holiday Camp. *J. Kiggia Kimani*
The Gamblers. *Julius Namale*
Colour of Carnations. *Ayub Ndii*
Son of Fate. *John Kiriamiti*

The Girl from Uganda

Tengio Urrio

EAST AFRICAN EDUCATIONAL PUBLISHERS
NAIROBI

Published by
East African Educational Publishers Limited
Brick Court
Mpaka Road/Woodvale Grove
Westlands
P.O. Box 45314
NAIROBI.

© Tengio Urrio
Published 1993
ISBN 9966-46-965-6

Printed by
Kenya Litho Limited
P.O. Box 40775, Nairobi.

This novel is dedicated to my mum and dad who helped me with a million and one things, among them was to read and write. And to my daughters, Zawadi Rosaline, Lulu Imelda and Kara Magdalene, who have contributed so much to my happiness.

Prologue

Life in a Western city can be very lonely, not only to a foreigner but even to a local person. The tempo of life is exhausting. Nobody readily talks to you and no one really cares. Neighbours pass without noticing each other, and faces have no ready smiles, but sneers. Foreigners are looked down upon and the black man is considered inferior to other races. This is the society I lived in and, like many people in it, I was nearly driven to insanity and suicide. Plucked from a small city in Africa, near my little primitive village, primitive by Western standards but most civilized compared to what I see happening in this foreign city. There is suicide, murder, rape, drug addiction, alcoholism, racism - you name it. I just could not cope with life until I met Betty.

I lived with Betty for six months. The moment I met her she became not just a friend but a true friend. She played the role of everything to me - a companion, a lover, a cook and an advisor. I admired, loved and honoured her as a member of my family. She was an angel – a God sent guardian angel who came into my life when I needed her most.

In this world where people are no longer interested in each other, where no man wants to help another one in time of need, there are very few Bettys. Husbands and wives fight, children and parents are at each other's throats. Brothers "knife" each other and the man in the street, though he may not know you, passes you with a sneer, because of God knows what!

Betty was none of these. She was the nicest person I had ever met. But as it happens to all nice people, the flame of life did not burn in her for too long. It was extinguished prematurely before shining long enough to show me the way in this dark world. A world where the fit survive at the expense of the weak, and the wicked live longer than the humble.

As I write this story I feel hollow inside me. I am not sure whether I will finish this story because tears are already welling up in my eyes, and I cannot see very well. The page I am writing on is soaked with tear drops and I am sobbing and shivering with cold in this lonely apartment. It is as if I am inside a deep freezer, as it is winter time and downstairs they have turned down the thermostat to save fuel, because the energy crisis has apparently hit the most developed country in the world.

But I will not stop writing. I must keep on writing because I promised Betty that I would write this story. I will therefore write on and on, cry and cry, but I will not stop until I fulfil my promise of writing about the frustration of living in an alien country.

Betty saved my life and sanity and that is why I am missing her so much. I miss her all the time. I am lonely in this alien land. I am cold and empty, so much so that I feel like dying, because no human mind can withstand the loss I have suffered, the loss of the only person I cherished and loved, and being left alone in this alien country. But I must write on. I am sure I will finish the story because I am not writing it alone. I am writing it with Betty. I trust she is with me, because in between my crying bouts, like an orphaned child, I remember her last words.

"Fred, I love you, and if you truly love me as you say you do, do not allow my death to drive you to a mental hospital."

Chapter 1

Son of the soil

It was like watching a movie. A barefooted boy wearing an old school uniform was walking down a narrow footpath. It looked as if it had rained the previous night as the ground was wet with mud and the grass encroaching on the path had lots of dew.

The boy tried to hurry but the mud was slowing down his speed. The further he went the more mud he collected. It stuck to the underside of his feet and made him look like he was wearing platform shoes. From the underside of his feet some of the mud squeezed in between his large toes and reappeared on the upper side of the toes in what looked like thin sausages. The boy kept on plodding along, hurriedly.

The morning dew washed the lower parts of his legs and dropped on the mud on the upper side of his feet, giving them a shiny look.

Protruding from the front pocket of his khaki shorts was a half eaten piece of maize. It looked as if it had been roasted the previous night. It seemed he had eaten half of it for his breakfast and kept the other half to serve as his snack during school break.

The boy arrived at the school. The large board in front of the school read, *Kideleko Primary School*. A tall teacher, a stick in hand, was standing near the board. By the look on his face the boy was late and he was going to be punished. He held the boy by his shirt and gave him strong strokes on his buttocks. No wonder his shorts were wearing out at the seats. It looked as if this was his only school uniform and it was wearing away at the buttocks because of the constant beatings.

The scene now changed. I saw a gentleman clad in a

Kaunda suit getting out of the back seat of the black Mercedes Benz. He wore expensive shoes that looked like those you see in the duty free shops in airports in Europe. He had a Samsonite briefcase in his right hand. The other hand held a file. I could read the letters on the file: "TANZANIA GOVERNMENT."

The person stretched, waved the driver off and walked into a posh house. It was at this time that I saw his face. He resembled the boy I saw walking barefoot to school. Apart from a well kept beard the face resembled very much that of the boy. It was one and the same person alright. Wanting to see more I rubbed my eyes. The act of rubbing my eyes seemed to have switched off the "movie."

I woke up to find myself seated in my office chair in the Ministry of National Economy headquarters in Dar es Salaam. The first thing I saw was a large envelope on my desk. Miriam, my secretary, had walked into my office when I was asleep and placed it on my table with the sender's address on the top. It read, "From the Dean– Massachusetts College of Economics."

I looked at my large golden watch, the time was 11 a.m. No wonder I had slept. I used to sleep in my office almost everyday between 10 a.m. and 11 a.m. for about half an hour. During this time, my secretary would not let anybody enter my office and she would not allow any telephone calls. Please do not think that I slept in the office because I was lazy, far from it. I slept because I often slept late after working overtime in the house trying to finish the day's office work. Whenever I woke up from the half sleep in my office I would feel better, brighter and strong enough to continue working till late in the afternoon.

This morning's sleep was deeper than usual, perhaps because I was more tired than the other mornings. I slept so deeply that I had a dream in which I dreamt about my early childhood.

4

My name is Fred Munyao. I was born of very poor peasant parents in Kideleko village in Muheza District, in Tanga Region, Tanzania. I went to Kideleko Primary School.

In those days going to school was the exception rather than the rule, and my father sent me to school to get me away from the home compound where I used to play the whole day while refusing to do any work. He sent me to school not because he believed that getting educated was important. Far from that, he sent me to school because as he said, I needed "to be taught some manners." He believed that only the teacher's stick at Kideleko Primary School could straighten the crooked boy that I was those days. He had seen a teacher who did not spare the cane, and thought that was exactly what a notorious and useless boy like me needed!

We were poor, very poor. My father, God bless him, sold coconuts in order to buy school uniform for me, which I wore during my four years in primary school. It was the only uniform I had. Often, during inspection time at school, the teacher would cane me for having a dirty uniform. Why didn't he try to wear the same uniform everyday and see what would happen to it? Of course I could not ask him. Nobody dared talk to or ask him anything. Whenever I got caned, I would return home with sore buttocks, wash my uniform and hang it above the fire over which my mother used to prepare the evening meal that consisted of cassava boiled in coconut milk. I would leave the uniform there overnight and the next day I would find it a little wet. But I would still wear it and let it dry on me on my way to school.

My father had thought I was going to run away from school but for some reason I preferred the teacher's cane to working on my father's cassava farm. When we did the Standard IV examination I got top marks and was allowed to enter Standard V at Kideleko Middle School. The middle school was in my village. It was a boarding school so I moved to the school, although our house was only three miles away. I could have walked everyday to the school as I had done previously but, the headmaster insisted that middle school pupils had to stay at the school.

My father bought me a second school uniform. I now had two school uniforms. He had by now realized that I was a bright boy because only bright boys got themselves accepted into Kideleko Middle School, the only middle school in Muheza District. He would have liked to buy shoes but he could not afford. The money he got from selling coconuts and cassava was barely enough to buy food, let alone shoes and clothes.

It was when I entered St. Andrew's College, Minaki, that I wore my first pair of shoes. That does not mean that we were now financially better off. I would for example leave home with only twenty shillings that was not enough to buy soap for the five-month long term. Although the school was 16 miles from the city of Dar es Salaam, and I would have loved to visit the city more often, I could not afford the fare on the *Hapa-Jee?* buses that plied between Manerumango in Kisarawe and Dar es Salaam. But I used to go there at least once a term. On my return home, my friends in the village always inquired about the city of Dar es Salaam that none of them had seen. They thought that because my school's address was P.O. Box 28004, Dar es Salaam, the school was situated in the centre of the city. In order to have something to tell them, I would visit Dar es Salaam at least once every term.

Because I could not afford the fare to the city I would walk all the way from Minaki to Ukonga. This saved me three shillings. From Ukonga I would pay only two shillings to Dar es Salaam.

The only place I knew and visited during those few trips into the city of Dar es Salaam, was the area around Mnazi Mmoja. I did not have to go very far because I got all that I needed in Mnazi Mmoja, like sight seeing and a two shilling dish of "Biriani" rice at Tanganyika Hotel, near the present Lumumba Primary School, opposite Mnazi Mmoja Dispensary.

During the holidays, in my village, I used to impress my agemates who had not been to the city, that I knew the city like the back of my hand.

"I have even shaken hands with the Governor, Sir Edward Twining, whom we have the chance of seeing almost every week," I would add.

When I joined Form Five at Minaki I wore my first pair of trousers. They were tailored at Kichwele Tailoring Mart, again at Mnazi Mmoja. Kichwele Tailoring Mart that sold me my first pair of trousers for sixty shillings is still there on what is now Uhuru Street, that was then Kichwele Street.

The terylene trousers were perhaps the best tailored "material" I have ever worn in my life.

From St. Andrew's College, Minaki, I went to Makerere University College in Kampala, Uganda, where I graduated with a Bachelor's Degree in Economics. On my return home I was employed as an Economist in the Ministry of National Economy and earned my way up through hard work, to the post of Assistant Principal Secretary, the third in charge at the Ministry that plans the economy of the nation.

Chapter 2

The Scholarship

After what seemed like eternity, the letter from Massachusetts College of Economics had arrived at last. I had been accepted for a Master's Degree programme in Economics in one of the most prestigious colleges in U.S.A., a school considered by many prominent economists as the Mecca of American and European Economists. The school fall semester was starting in two weeks time. The letter said I was to report for registration and orientation as soon as possible. I realized that I had to move fast if I was to make it to Boston, Massachusetts, U.S.A. on time. The letter said that there would be a ten dollar fine for late registration and it did not mention that an Assistant Principal Secretary would be exempted from paying the fine if he came late. I guessed I had better move fast.

Chief, the Principal Secretary in the Ministry of National Economy where I was an Assistant Principal Secretary, had called me to his office one Monday morning. Chief rarely called me to his office. He would usually telephone unless it was something that required a lengthy discussion. But we rarely had problems that required lengthy discussion. Our decisions and implementations were always prompt and efficient.

"Look," he had said, "the World Bank wants us to send one of our staff members to the United States to study for a Master's Degree in Economics."

"That is very fine Chief," I said. "I will suggest a couple of possible candidates. We have a good number of bright boys and girls working with us. We should be able to choose the most intelligent and hard working." I always liked to give a clear and concise answer.

Chief did not look impressed by my answer though. "You seem to have revised the principles of management recently - management by incentives, upward mobility and all that stuff." Chief was sure in a good mood that morning. This could have been due to the fact that Chief, unlike many of us never suffered from the Monday morning syndrome because he never drank alcohol, and I guess that is how he got to be the Principal Secretary, through hard work and no booze.

"You know too well that most of the boys and girls you are talking about have only recently returned from universities with their "Born Again" or "Born Afresh Degrees", whatever you call those degrees they hand out in hundreds these days. During our time, they used to issue only diplomas. And we were only twenty five in the whole university."

"Bachelor of Arts, you mean!" I interrupted. "Never mind what I mean," he continued in a more serious tone. These boys should sit behind those desks, and be given an opportunity to contribute to national development before the nation invests any more of the tax payers' money in them."

Talking of patriotism, Chief was very patriotic. "O.K., I will look around, perhaps in our up-country stations, I will find someone who is qualified, leave it to me." I was getting impatient although I did not show it. Monday morning 9 a.m. discussing a small problem of choosing one out of fifty qualified staff to go and read for a Master's Degree. Put the names in a hat, tell one of the office sweepers to pick out a candidate. Who cares? After all, I had no Master's Degree and I was doing pretty well as an Assistant Principal Secretary, and I was the third in charge, in the Ministry of National Economy!

Chief did not realize that our brains did not function too well on Monday mornings till after the ten o'clock tea. Why didn't he try to drink even one beer on Sunday and see?

Perhaps his brain would not function effectively for a whole week.

"I wish I was young again and ready to go to school. I sure would not let this chance pass by. I would grab it, go to U.S.A., be a student for a year and earn a Master's Degree - Fred Munyao, Master in Economics," I gaffed hoping that he would let me go back to my office. I was sure by now Miriam, my beautiful secretary, was waiting for me with the morning tea and home made cakes. We always had tea together whenever I was around. This created the spirit of good working relationship.

"Actually, I think you should go," he said. This time he looked at me straight in the eyes. He looked happy as if he had just solved a big problem which if left unsolved, would have pushed the nation into bankruptcy. "I am sure we shall manage without you till you come back, after all, it is only one year."

I thought he was joking.

"You need a Master's Degree to keep ahead," he continued. "You see all these kids coming from overseas universities with Master's Degrees and working under you may not give you the respect you deserve. Although of course with your B.A. Economics degree and your experience, you definitely know more than they do, and perhaps more than they will ever know," he added shrugging his shoulders.

Chief had very little respect for the existing system of education. He used to think his diploma in Business Administration was superior to my degree in Economics. He did not attempt to hide his lack of confidence in the younger elite.

"You have been working your tail off for quite sometime. Take a break, go away to U.S.A., away from this mind boggling job. You do not have to learn or study very hard when you get to the States. You know all these things, you will certainly pass the exams with the least effort and you will enjoy yourself too. There will be parties, good people, and girls – oh! Yeah! The girls! You are young and still a bachelor, you might even meet your future wife there! American girls are very nice and understanding. Who knows you might come back married. Things have changed these days. It is not like in the old days when you had to be married to a girl of your own race and tribe. People are going overseas to study and they come back with two certificates – one academic, the other marital."

Amidst protests, he called Joyce, his secretary and dictated a letter:

"The World Bank, Washington, U.S.A. In reply to your letter I hereby submit the application forms for Fred Munyao for consideration by the World Bank, to enable him to study for a Master's Degree in Economics . . ."

Then followed lots and lots of kind words about my character and performance on the job, some of which were true and some of which were an extreme exaggeration of the reality.

In fact Chief was right. I mean he was right about the usefulness of a Master's Degree , but I found it difficult to go back to school. I guess nobody in my position would have found it easy to agree to go back to school. With an air conditioned office on the eleventh floor of the Ministry of National Economy building, who would want to go back to school?. From here, I commanded the view of the Indian Ocean. I had a beautiful secretary, a three bedroomed government quarter at Msasani Peninsula, a living-in house servant, lots of good friends and a good time in and around the city, and last, but not least an important and responsible job as an Assistant Principal Secretary in the Ministry of National Economy.

What more did I want in this life? Who in my position would have been enthusiastic about going to live in Boston as a student for a whole year? Who would have agreed to sit in a classroom, to do exams and homework, do all what students do, and in a foreign land for a whole twelve months? Two months would be tolerable I guessed, but twelve months would be ten months too many. A few months, yes, a study tour for a few weeks travelling as a government executive like Chief used to do often, yes, but not a whole year of classwork and far away from home and friends, I thought.

My job as an Assistant Principal Secretary took me to several countries, but mainly to Europe and Asia. I had travelled to many European and Asian countries. I had even been to Russia, China and New Zealand, but I had not been to U.S.A. And I certainly had not been away from home at any one time for more than two months.

Between the day I applied for the scholarship and the day I received the letter of acceptance, my idea about going away to school had changed completely. Every time I opened a letter, it was a mind-splitting operation. I had expected to hear the news of my acceptance any time from the time I applied because Chief had indicated that with his contacts in U.S.A. the application would be processed promptly and in my favour. Chief kept on telling me about how envious he was of me, envious because I was going to have a lot of fun in U.S.A., in the land of socialising, that land where there are two cars parked in every garage, and two chickens in every cooking pot. He seemed to know the country like the back of his hand. And who was I to say he was wrong? He had been to U.S.A. several times, while I had not.

In fact Chief loved travelling to U.S.A. so much so that whenever there was an official trip to U.S.A., he would never let me go, he would always go himself. He used to say something about big economic deals and negotiations with a superpower that required his own personal attention. But rumour mongers thought otherwise. It was rumoured that he

12

grabbed every opportunity to travel to U.S.A. in order to contact his friend at the World Bank Headquarters in Washington. He liked living overseas and was looking forward to working with the World Bank at their offices in Washington, on retirement. He was 52 years old, so he had only three more years to go before retiring.

One thing had acted as a big inducement for me to accept the scholarship. Chief had hinted to me that on his retirement, and on my return from U.S.A. with a Master's Degree I would be the obvious candidate for his job.

"You have my blessings. I will put it in writing in the files," he had assured me. "You are a workaholic, Fred, and that is what this job demands. So keep it up and the job will be yours."

I had began to walk away when he added, "And one more thing. This job demands less drinking, or if you can help it, no drinking at all, and no messing around with secretaries, it is unethical and unprofessional."

For his sake I added, "Or if you can help it no messing around at all times and at all places."

With that, I walked to Miriam's office to see if she had finished typing the speech I was to deliver the next day at the Annual Convention of the East African Economists Association.

Back in my office that day I could not concentrate on reading my speech. I began thinking seriously about the Master's Degree and about Chief's job. "What is one year of school compared to being appointed Principal Secretary, Ministry of National Economy for Life?" I thought quietly. "If Idi Amin with only four years of schooling could appoint himself President for Life why not appoint myself Principal Secretary for Life, with my Master's Degree in Economics?"

Chief's job was good, a very good job indeed. It carried lots of responsibilities and lots of privileges and 'rights' too. Along with the job came a moderately good salary, a chauffeured Mercedes and numerous overseas trips. But of course, in turn the job required a lot of hard work, and what Chief called a high moral character, both of which I had, or thought I had. I seemed to have acquired them congenitally or perhaps they were built into me much earlier on in life.

I liked everything about Chief's job; everything except his secretary. Joyce was too serious for my liking and serious people, just like lazy people, do not appeal to me. Of course I had nothing against her, nothing at all, except her seriousness and lack of charm. She was pretty, hard working and a decently married lady. She was pretty in her own way but she was serious and nothing puts me off as a serious secretary. You see, the job of a secretary requires more than pretty dresses, typewriters, files, painted nails and hard work. It requires smiles, charm and the ability to put people at ease. Joyce did not put me at ease. I, an Assistant Principal Secretary was not at ease with her. Nurses know very well what I am talking about. Theirs is not only a profession of pretty girls in white uniforms, carrying syringes and needles and wheeling patients along hospitals corridors. They also smile, are nice and comforting to their patients and those they work with.

Miriam, unlike Joyce, was charming, exceedingly charming! On my return from U.S.A. Miriam would be the new personal secretary to the new Principal Secretary. I had decided.

Despite his morals and principles, Chief admired Miriam. There was nothing wrong with that of course. Her charm, beauty, pretty clothes and hard work would have won admiration from any man or from any woman for that matter. "She is always on top of things. Ask her anything in this office and she will either give you the information off head or will dig it up from the files in no time." Chief used to say of her.

I was sure that even Chief preferred Miriam to Joyce for

a secretary . That is why I thought, before I even get off the plane in Boston Chief would already be saying, "Goodbye Joyce, welcome Miriam." For sure Chief wanted Miriam for a secretary, and as I was leaving his office that morning after filling in the application forms for the scholarship, he asked, "How is Miriam this morning?" I did not answer. I pretended not to have heard him and kept on walking past the unsmiling Joyce in the outer office hammering away at her typewriter and into Miriam's office, smiled at her and went into my office to contemplate how I would miss my work, my office and Miriam, if I got the scholarship.

All things considered, Micky Nyambo was a good boss to work for. He was understanding, hard working and demanded nothing short of the best performance from those who worked under him, but he loved us all, especially Joyce, Miriam and I, with whom he worked very closely. That is why Miriam and I called him Chief. He was just like those old respectable chiefs of old days. In fact it was rumoured that he was the grandson of Chief Rukonge of Ukerewe. The rest of the staff members used to simply call him Mzee. At first, he did not like to be called Chief.

"It sounds too colonial," he complained. But we stuck to the name. However, we were careful not to refer to him as Chief when there were people around, although talking about colonial mentality, Chief used to dress in white suits when he was in the office, just like the colonial administrators and he insisted on working strictly by the Standing Orders that were established by the Colonial Administrators.

"If a worker is lazy or comes to work late without satisfactory explanation, fire him or her immediately," he used to say.

* * *

After I had read the letter of acceptance to Massachusetts College of Economics, I sat for quite a while in my rotating

15

chair thinking about all that I was leaving behind. Finally I decided that whatever I was leaving behind, I had a million more things waiting for me in U.S.A., as Chief had indicated. So the news was definitely worth celebrating. I was intending to celebrate as soon as I got over the painful process of explaining to Miriam that I was going away. Yeah! Miriam would miss me. We had a very good working relationship. My cook Juma Mohammed and his family would miss me too and I would definitely miss them. We lived like one big family. I began to pace aimlessly in my spacious office, while momentarily admiring the new Persian carpet on the floor. The day I had it delivered Chief joked about reporting me to the Minister for National Economy for misuse of public funds, but later changed his mind, and told me to order one for his office too. He correctly realized that the boss's office should be the most cosy in the Ministry.

I admired the modern furniture, the painting on the walls and the various souvenirs that I had accumulated during my six years of occupying the post of Assistant Principal Secretary. Some of the souvenirs I had were from the various countries I had travelled to in Asia and Europe, and others were gifts from my friends in Tanzania.

Finally I stopped at the window. The silk curtains were drawn. There was beautiful weather outside and a cold breeze was blowing in from the Indian Ocean. I looked below at the blue sea. The sea was quiet that morning. At a distance, at Kivukoni, I could see fishermen returning from their overnight fishing. House wives and house servants waited with empty baskets on the beach looking at the fishing boats with enthusiasm and hope. They reminded me of the American Indians looking out to the sea and on seeing the Columbus ships, wondered, but could not understand the significance of their arrival. That was the day the

America I was going to was opened up to the outside world.

I looked out in the harbour, there was a fleet of fifteen ships waiting to off-load goods brought in from various ports around the world. "Some of them could even be from California, San Francisco, New York, Boston! Who knows?" I thought!

Soon my mind began to wander. I forgot completely about the office behind my back, the place that had been like home to me for six good years. It was no longer important to me, my mind was in Boston, Massachusetts, in the "land of unlimited opportunities", as Chief had called it, and I thought of the good life waiting for me. The discos, the movies – oh yes! I will enjoy the uncensored movies. Chief had said that in U.S.A., they never censor movies. He said that in America, censoring was like being against the first amendment of their Constitution, if I can remember well. I thought about the parties I would attend. I had heard that Americans were very sociable and whenever they met a foreigner they always said, "We will get together soon, I will give you a ring." I thought of the bars I would sit in, drinking with American friends. Bars that had never closed since they opened the day Columbus's ships anchored on the American shores. I thought of the girls, girls of all colours! Oh yes! The girls! I will resurrect my long buried romantic life. I had been going celibate for a while under the banner of good morals. I will of course get myself a Mzungu girl. I had had lots of girls of my race when I was an active member of society. This time I would want to experience love from a Mzungu girl!

I was quite sure that I was in for a very good time.
U.S.A.! Washington! New York! The big apple! Boston Massachusetts College of Economics! American girls! Here I come. I am fully ready for you. Of course I do not have to ask whether or not you are ready for me. I know you are! I have been told and read about you. You are great! I am not

coming to prove your greatness. I am not a doubting Thomas. I am coming just to enjoy myself in the land of the free, the rich, the friendly, the land of unlimited opportunities . . ., I longingly thought to myself.

The telephone rang. It seemed exceptionally loud that morning. This does not mean that I was annoyed to be disturbed out of my fantasy. I then thought that it was not normal for a mentally sound person to stand by a window at ten o'clock in the morning, day dreaming like a psychiatric patient.

"Fred, would you like to have a cup of coffee first or would you rather go through those files on your table? There is some stuff that Chief wants you to go through quickly and give him feedback. He would like you to examine the position of the on-going Swedish International Development Agency-funded projects. This work is overdue. I have just finished talking to Chief's secretary and, she says that Chief would like to present the report to the minister before the end of this week," said Miriam. Her voice was a bit hoarse that morning.

"Damn it!" I thought, she must have been out last night drinking and dancing the *Kamanyola* with her Swedish boyfriend. Possibly they were at Mpakani Bar dancing and having a nice time the whole night. Perhaps she did not sleep a wink last night.

I did not understand why I was jealous. Her private life was no business of mine, but still there I was, as jealous as a college sophomore. Well, Stephan Nielsen, her Swedish boyfriend who was working in the Ministry of Health, was far away from home, and being so far away from home he was bound to be lonely, unless he found himself a good girl, and Miriam happened to be one. I could not blame Stephan Nielsen for being in love with Miriam, assuming that he was in love. If Miriam was not my secretary, and if I did not put my morals and my job in the same basket, I would have been

18

running after Miriam myself. I thought I really should not have been all that jealous because after all I was going to U.S.A., far from home. Who then will blame me, if I too will have an American girlfriend, possibly one of my class-mates. I am told that in America women go to school in their millions, so you end up going to school with a lot of pretty girls. We will explore the city together, walk in the parks, go to movies, discos, walk the Freedom Trail, go to New York's Madison Square, Statue of Liberty and visit museums and the many places of historical importance in and around the city of Boston. We definitely will have good time!

"Fred, are you there?" Miriam sounded impatient. My mind was certainly not on the job. I was already in Boston. The thousands of miles return journey took only a split of a second. "Oh, yes!" I said. In fact I had already forgotten what she had said, and I was about to tell her to come to the office so that I could break the news gently to her when she interrupted.

"I am sorry, just a minute, Chief is on the line, talk to him then I will bring in the coffee tray, O.K.?" I did not answer because for the first time, I was in no mood for Miriam's mothering. My mind was in Boston, Massachusetts, U.S.A.

Micky's strong voice came on the phone, loud and clear, in fact too loud as usual. Chief always talked on the phone as if he was talking to someone in Iceland. He could practically rupture your ear drum and dislocate your ossicles if you talked to him with the ear piece too close to your auditory apparatus. While talking to him on the phone, I would always hold the phone with the ear piece a foot away from the ear, so that I would let the unnecessary sound waves dissipate in the air and only tap the amount required for transmitting the message.

"Congratulations, Fred. You made it! You made it! I have just received a letter from the World Bank saying that you should be released immediately. This is great! Fred

Munyao, Master's in Economics is no longer a dream. It is now a reality and, just imagine all the good time waiting for you in the U.S.A.," Chief rattled.

I could have killed him. I mean for discussing it on the phone because I did not want Miriam to know that I was going away. I wanted to gently break the news to her myself. Now the secret was known. While Chief was talking to me, she was listening in us as usual. She always listened in on us when I was talking to Chief on the phone. It was a time saving and efficiency promoting arrangement I had made with her. It saved her time and mine because if she heard what Chief wanted done, then I would not have to explain to her. She would go ahead and dig up the information required. Often, she reminded me about the tasks if I forgot or was held up by other duties. It was only when we were discussing highly confidential matters, or very personal affairs that Miriam would not be allowed to listen in, in which case then, I would press a button on my desk and her receiver would go dead. I always imagined the look on her face as she put down the receiver whenever I pressed the button. But Miriam did not mind, it was something we had agreed upon. This time I had forgotten to press the button. Definitely my mind was not on the job.

Chief continued to congratulate me and finished with, "If you need any more information about life in U.S.A. just give me a call or ask Joyce to look into my schedule, and see when we can sit and have a longer chat concerning life and pleasure in U.S.A."

I was going to say, "Over a bottle of beer of course." I however, remembered in time that I was talking to a member of alcoholics anonymous, so I added politely, "Thanks, Chief."

"You are welcome," he answered.
While I always said a simple, "Not at all", after a "thank you," Chief always came out with, "You are welcome." I

used to think that it was a direct translation from the Swahili "*karibu bwana*", said after good-bye. I did not bother to ask him whether or not he was speaking English in Kiswahili or the other way round. I was to discover later, that while in England they say "not at all", in America, they say "You are welcome." This showed that Chief was Americanised to some extent.

No sooner had I finished talking to Chief than Miriam stormed into the office. She did not bring the coffee. She brought tears, lots and lots of tears. She had tears everywhere in her eyes, on her eye lashes, on her cheeks. All over her face! A tear drop as large as a marble, sat precariously on her left cheek, threatening to fall off any time as she inhaled and exhaled in distress. It is not easy to appreciate how many litres of tears we have stored in our eyes waiting to well up when the occasion demands. However, I still did not think my going away deserved that many tears.

I had not seen Miriam cry before, in fact I had not seen anybody cry for a long time. Seeing Miriam crying pained me. But I did not know how to make her stop. I had not realized that she cared so much about me. Her crying spoiled my happiness and longing for going to U.S.A.

"Miriam please, control yourself or go home and rest or something. You do not realize how much suffering you cause me by your crying. Why are you crying, anyway?" I said putting on the Assistant Principal Secretary look.

She sat down, wiped the tears off, peered into a mirror and she was herself again, the Miriam I knew, the Miriam I had worked with for six years without ever getting on each others nerves.

"You still have not told me what you were crying for?" I repeated smiling, having nothing else to say.

"Nothing, really, afterall crying does not help and that will not stop you from going to U.S.A. I wonder if I shall ever get another person to work with as happily as I enjoyed working with you," she said.

I just sat there looking into empty space. What was I supposed to say. This was one morning when my mind was not working too well. Maybe it was because I had not had my morning tea. If this happens during a lecture at Massachusetts College of Economics, I would have to walk out and get a cup of tea or something. I hoped that they had coffee served in between or even during lectures. After all, we would be graduate students and sitting in a lecture room in the land of unlimited opportunities, they would have coffee served by waiters in chefs' uniforms in between lectures, I thought to myself.

"Why didn't you tell me that you had applied for a scholarship to go to study in U.S.A.?" Miriam asked.

I explained to her that at the beginning it did not seem that important, I was not that enthusiastic to go, but then now, I could not wait to get there.

"Didn't Joyce tell you that I had applied for a scholarship?"

"Oh, no! She thinks everything is confidential," she replied. The two secretaries were not very fond of each other.

"I will miss you, I enjoyed working with you. I owe a lot of what I have to you. By giving me so much encouragement and responsibility you made me develop the spirit of hard work and ambition to get ahead," she said.

Miriam was right. When she got assigned to me she had no experience at all, let alone the education, to qualify to be my personal secretary. But in no time, she had learnt to run the office single handedly. She was better than me in many respects. Her quick realisation that hard work, orderly and disciplined work, was the only way to get going increased the efficiency at the Ministry to everybody's satisfaction. Even Chief was impressed. Usually it was not easy to please him. To please him you had to stop boozing, visit the mosque or church several times a day and, spend all of your working hours in the office.

"When will you return from U.S.A.?"

"After one year. Long time isn't it? I will probably find you married." It seemed as if subconsciously I did not want her to get married. Why? I could not tell.

"You will enjoy yourself very much in U.S.A. You will perhaps get married, too," she teased me, with a giggle.

"You will get married." I returned. The conversation was not getting us anywhere, so she left me reading the instructions that accompanied the letter of admission.

"Do you still want to know why I was crying?" she later asked.

"Yes," I said.

"I love you," she announced.

Miriam was stating a fact. She loved me, and I loved her too, but we never admitted it to each other. However, our love was not the "boss loves secretary kind of thing." This was true love, loving a person for what they are. It was more than love, it was admiration, care for each other, being intimately involved in what the other person does. It was a sister-brother love affair, for lack of better description. Nobody could blame us for developing such a relationship. Try working with a nice person for six years and see. It was admiration for a person, because that person happens to be an exceptional person. It was a unique working relationship, where we worked hard together, and got things done, promptly and efficiently.

People in the office used to whisper about us, but they got tired of it when they realised that, our relationship was mere friendship, almost like that between a father and a daughter. After all, the way I treated her was not different from the way I treated anybody else in the ministry. I was friendly and loved everybody who was hard working.

We all loved each other very much. We were a team. But with Miriam the relationship was more personal. For example, during our half hour coffee break, we would spend ten minutes discussing the day's work. Then we would get on to more interesting things about Miriam's love life, and talk about the rumours and the talk of the city, to get our minds off the job for a while. Miriam knew about what was going on in the city more than I did. She used to tell me things that made me wonder why she did not get herself a job with the Tanzania News Agency. When it came to what was left of my love life, she was like a sister to me. She would advise me on which girls to go with because she knew personal histories of so many girls, and she would always try to shelter me from what she referred to as "the bad girls." She used to remind me that my love life needed some beefing up. "You are wasting the best years of your life. There are beautiful chicks dying to be loved by you."

I would simply answer: "No way."

The news of my getting a scholarship spread like wild fire through the offices of the ministry.

"Do you know Fred is going to America to do a Masters Degree?" People kept on asking each other. The telephone kept on ringing, people congratulating me. In the corridors, everybody I met shook hands with me to congratulate me. It looked as if I had won a lottery ticket. Even my office messenger came in to say, "Mzee, I wish you all the best."

I could not stand it any more. I was a little confused. The news was overwhelming. I telephoned my boss to say that I was taking the day off.

He told me, "Take the day off and stay away, until the day you come back with your Master's Degree from U.S.A."

I bid Miriam farewell, leaving the letter of instructions with her, knowing that she would understand it better than I could. She would then get all the necessary documents on time – the visa, vaccination certificate, the air ticket –

everything. She would use her "contacts" if necessary.

From the office I went to the Hotel Skyway lounge. The barman welcomed me with, "Look who is here at this hour. The A.P.S., a critic of those who drink during office hours!"

I had to justify my being there at 1 p.m. , and so I replied that I was no longer the A.P.S. I was going to be a student in U.S.A.

They say if you want news to spread tell it to a woman, but barmen are just as good at spreading news. Everybody who came to the bar that afternoon was told of my impending journey to U.S.A. Those who knew me, and those who did not know me bought beer to celebrate, and for the first time in many years I downed eight bottles of Safari beer.

At around 7 p.m. I felt I could not drink any more. The manager of Hotel Skyway, who was a personal friend, got a car to take me home. Popularity and friendship come in handy when you are tipsy in a bar, therefore, I decided to get home before I made a fool of myself.

As I fumbled with the key to my Msasani Peninsula house, Juma came from the servant quarters. He always woke up to serve my supper even if I came home after midnight, but often I would send him away. Sometimes I decided to serve myself supper.

Tonight he had left roast lamb, chips and rice cooked in coconut milk in the oven and it was still warm. Juma was the best cook around. He had twenty years cooking experience behind him. He used to cook for a colonial administrator during those days. Now he was my cook, living in the servant quarters adjoining my house with his third wife, a son and a grown up daughter, Helen.

Tonight I had a voracious appetite. I ate the chips, rice and lamb. I thought the piece of lamb was too small, but I consoled myself with, "You'll have lots of lamb, in U.S.A."

Chapter 3

Arrival in Boston

"Ladies and gentlemen, the captain has put on the 'no smoking' sign and we shall be landing at Boston's Logan Airport in a short while. Please stay in your seats until we are ready to deplane. The time in Boston is 8.00 p.m. and the temperature is 45 degrees Fahrenheit. We will take off for San Francisco in an hour's time. Those proceeding to San Francisco can wait in the plane or in the Airport lounge until we are ready to board, those disembarking, please find your way through the customs. Thank you for flying Lufthansa, goodbye, and have a nice evening." The beautiful German accent signed off.

I had dozed off for a while despite my efforts not to. I had tried my best to keep awake and enjoy the beautiful white clouds and the blue sea through the eight hour flight from London. But I guess I must have dozed off because of the champagne I had drank, or maybe I was beginning to suffer from jet lag even before I reached my destination. It was 8.00 p.m. in Boston. Back home in Dar es Salaam it must have been 2.00 a.m. many hours past my sleeping time.

I looked out of the window. We were still flying above the sea, but ahead I could see the city of Boston. It looked like a sea of buildings of various colours and heights. Although it was 8.00 p.m. the sun had just set, leaving the city with the beautiful colour of sunset which reflected from the buildings. They made a very spectacular view from above. Added to this, were the clouds that hovered above the city. A thin line of clouds engulfed the buildings barely covering them. It was a sight probably appreciated only by those landing in Boston for the first time, but anybody with a sense of appreciation for nature could definitely not miss it. Above the city two sky scrapers, the Prudential Hotel and the John Hancock Tower jutted out into the sky above all the other buildings, like two out-stretched arms saying, "welcome to Boston." More sea, oil refineries, land...we landed. Twenty hours of travel had brought me from half way across the world, a total length of Columbus and Vasco da Gama's journey put together. I had finally arrived into what my boss had described as the land of unending happiness.

At the immigration, my passport underwent the usual close scrutiny. Americans are pretty careful at examining passports. They are checked fast and efficiently, but very thoroughly. This is because illegal immigrants have been entering the country in great numbers in recent times. People looking for the good life, freedom, jobs, fortunes. People running away from political strife and hunger in their countries, on hearing of the promise of a better life. Apparently, these people arrive in boats, ships, by air or even on foot, in their thousands. And the immigration people have to be extra careful to admit only those who have gone through the proper channels. People have been coming in from all countries. Mexico, Haiti, Indo-China, Vietnam, Nigeria and Ethiopia. They have found their way here in great numbers and still more are trying their best to find their way in.

The immigration official asked me, "What school are you going to?"

"Massachusetts College of Economics," I answered.

"Good school," he said, looking at me from inside the glass compartment. He had had his eyes on the papers all the time, but as soon as I mentioned Massachusetts School of Economics, it was as if I had mentioned that I was going to heaven on foot. He looked at me enviously and said, "Congratulations."

People were as cordial and charming just as Chief had

said. He punched the information on my passport into a computer and handed me my papers. The expiry date of the visa was very valuable information and would be in the computer's data bank until I left the country. If the expiry date arrived and I was still in U.S.A. the computer would show a red signal, and the immigration officials would be at my door with deportation papers. But of course, for a law abiding student like myself that would not occur, besides I must return home as soon as I graduate. I could not afford to wait for even a day because I was to return home and take up my job as soon as possible. What if Chief left his office and they were forced to choose somebody else to replace him when I was away? The thought frightened me. I decided that I would return as soon as I graduated, lest somebody else beats me to the job.

It took sometime to go through the luggage at the customs section, and I was glad to go outside into the cool evening air. A mild breeze was blowing. It must have rained in the afternoon, because the air smelt so nice. It was beautiful to arrive in Boston, at last.

The crowd was big, this being one of the points of entry into and exit from the country. I mixed with the crowd and soon found myself in a short queue waiting for taxis. The taxis were parked in a line down the street, so that a taxi would pull over to the ramp and the first person in the queue would get in. It would then drive off and the next taxi would pull over to pick the next person in the queue. Everything was orderly. As soon as you set your foot on the ramp the next taxi in the line pulls over and you are on your way home. It was not like in Dar es Salaam where taxi drivers pester you. They all want to take you to the same place at different fares! It was such a hassle. You do not know whether to go with the gentleman with the 404 for six hundred shillings or with the one driving a 504 for seven hundred shillings. However, both would want to take you to your destination.

After a little while it was my turn. I was at the ramp standing with my luggage on my side ready for the final leg of my journey in this great country. But there seemed to be a hitch in the process which had been running smoothly. No taxi pulled up. The driver in the taxi who was next on the queue was just staring into empty space, he did not pull up onto the ramp. "Maybe his taxi was out of order," I thought. But if it was out of order, the driver would bother to see what was wrong or he would ask for help to get it out of the way, and thus make way for the other taxis. But he was there, just staring into empty space. For sure there was nothing wrong with the taxi. I looked down the street at the driver behind the wheel. He was looking at me as if he was not seeing me. I felt a little embarrassed. Why was he not coming over? Was something wrong? There he was looking at me under his taxi driver's cap, but he was not coming over! I looked behind wanting to ask someone in the queue what was wrong and apologise if I was to blame. It seemed like the driver of that taxi was holding the queue. For sure it could not have been my mistake, because I did exactly what everybody else did. I walked up the ramp and waited for the taxi to pull over just as those ahead of me did!

I then noticed a funny expression on the faces of the people behind me. A gentleman who pretended to read a newspaper was not actually reading. He was looking at me over the top of the paper. Two ladies down the line looked down as if to show sympathy for the awkwardness of the situation. An elderly gentleman just stood there with that respectable look that comes with old age. All these people seemed to understand why the taxi driver did not come over. You could read it in their eyes. They were not completely ignorant of the situation I had found myself in.

I was going to ask, "Is there anything the matter?" But soon, the driver in the taxi second in line started his car, backed off a little, and then moved at a high speed. I thought he was going to stop ten miles away from the ramp, but he stopped with screeching brakes. He stopped near where I was standing, the car swung to and fro, and before it settled, he was out loading my suitcases into the booth hurriedly as if he was being chased by the police.

"Let's go, Brother," he said while shaking his head. The driver was an African American about twenty years old.

As we drove off, this time at reasonable speed the driver said, "Damn this white cabbies, they will not pick a black man even during the day. Damn racists, they think every black man lives in Roxbury and, they know if they go there at this hour they will have their asses whipped off."

I understood very little of what he said. I wanted to ask him what he meant by whites, blackmen, racists, Roxbury ... but I did not know how to ask or where to start. However, he seemed to assume that I understood what he was talking about. And if he assumed that I understood, well then I understood, and after all it was not difficult to understand what he was talking about. What he was saying, and he was right, which he assumed I knew, was that the white cab driver did not pull over to take me home because he was white and I was black, and he came to take me home because he was black and I was black. It was as plain as that, but it took me sometime to figure it out. I must confess that if he had not said it, I would have thought about it and then dismissed it as an unsolved and unimportant mystery.

"Where are you going man?" he asked with his left hand on the steering wheel and the right on the stereo selecting some music to make the journey enjoyable.

"The YMCA, I am told it is on Massachusetts Avenue." I replied.

"Shit! I have been waiting in the damn airport for hours and look at what I have got. A fare going within walking distance of the airport!"

"I was told it is five miles from the Airport", I said, not trying to argue or correct him, but trying to make sure of my destination.

"I have to make a buck man. I don't make no profits by taking fares going short distances. I cannot make any profit that way. I have to make a living, understand what I am saying?"

I stayed quiet because it seemed to me that a few moments to recapitulate on the mysteries that had taken place in the last five minutes might help. It helps you understand what goes on.

We drove up Hillman Road, through Perry's Avenue and down Pickwick Street. We were heading for the tunnel to get us out of the traffic full airport and into the city. But there was a holdup of the traffic at the entrance into the tunnel. "Must be a traffic jam," I thought. We were going almost at zero speed and behind us and in front of us cars stretched to infinity. Ahead of us, at the entrance into the tunnel, I heard shouts, slogans and singing. From our position I could not see the people properly but the placards they held way up in the air were conspicuously visible. "A demonstration, or a political rally," I thought.

"Those damn whites," the driver shouted certainly annoyed by the hold up of the traffic. "It has been like this for the last two weeks. These people can stay here and demonstrate for months, they have nothing to do, nothing to fear, being white they have the time and money stashed away in their banks to last them a lifetime. It is people like us who have to work our tails off. This is shit man! Understand what I am saying?"

We crawled at a snail's speed, slowly decreasing the distance between us and the entrance. Now I had a better view of the demonstrators. Men, women and children of all ages singing, chanting, walking quietly and carrying placards. Except for the fact that they were holding up traffic, it was a very orderly crowd. It seemed they were dissatisfied about something and at the same time it seemed some of them were having a nice time and enjoying the occasion. The motorists were definitely annoyed. You could tell by the way the drivers looked at them. Some were shouting at them while some just drove quietly negotiating their way through the crowd, or just stopping to wait and hope that there would appear by chance an opening in the crowd. There were two policemen in the crowd to see that nobody was hurt. I could now clearly read the placards. *"To hell with proposition two and a half; The Mayor must listen to his voters; we want more Police protection; we want more fire protection."*

Definitely the posters made sense, but I did not understand what "proposition two and a half" meant. So in order to break up the silence and to understand the situation I asked, "What is proposition two and a half?"

"This is a crazy city, man! Look at these whites demonstrating and causing inconveniences for everybody, just because two of their many policemen working in their neighbourhoods have been withdrawn. The city claims it has no money to pay them. The black neighbourhoods make do without police protection and fire protection, yet we do not take to the street and cause inconvenience. If the demonstrators were blacks, the police would have been here to hurl their asses away into prison. You cannot demonstrate and hold up traffic if you are black, that would be rioting, if you are white that is okay."

I decided that the conversation was going too far, I was getting more information that I was ready for. I could not yet understand these things so soon. I needed time. So I did not ask any more questions.

We were now at the entrance of the tunnel. We were still moving at a snail's pace in the middle of an ocean of cars. If the cab driver was complaining about the YMCA being within walking distance it was now within a crawling distance. The fare meter read six dollars and we were not a quarter way of the journey yet. The demonstrators were getting noisier and the drivers of the vehicles were getting more impatient. The drivers were slowly negotiating through the crowd. It needed a lot of patience and self control. Some of the drivers were trading insults with the demonstrators, but often the demonstrators would not answer back. They just marched, sang and withheld the traffic by blocking the entrance into the tunnel. They did not seem to care what the drivers called them, they were not there to hold a dialogue with drivers. Their aim was to have their demands known.

The driver ahead of us negotiated through the demonstrators. I did not think he was seeing in front of him because one of the demonstrators, a fat old man about fifty years sat on the bonnet of his car. This helped him in a way, as the demonstrators realized he did not see where he was going, and got out of his way while he drove blindly but carefully and found himself at the tunnel entrance. The fat man realizing that he was being carried right into the tunnel jumped off the car to the cheering of the crowd.

It was now our turn to go through the ordeal.
"If anybody sits on my car I will push his ass off," the cab driver said.

Everybody seemed to have his technique of getting through the demonstrators. Some would negotiate slowly through them. Some would beseech them to let them through, some would drive right through them and whoever did not want to get hurt had to move out of the way. And that is what we did. The driver pressed on the accelerator and took off. As soon as I held my breath thinking that he had hit someone, he stepped on the brakes and stopped at some person's foot, who by this time would be so shaken that they would just move out of the way, only to be replaced by another who would be treated the same way, but to our advantage. We gained our way through the demonstrators. I must say I was pretty shaken and scared. Really scared! I sat glued to my seat with the windows of the car securely closed. It seemed as if I was not going to make it to the YMCA, although the driver had said it was within a walking distance. All the time I thought "What would happen if we were to be involved in an accident? What would happen if the driver ran into one of the demonstrators and he or she got hurt? You never know with demonstrators, sometimes they get out of control. We might end up in a police station, in hospital or even at the city morgue. I had come from miles and miles away without an accident and here I was within walking distance to my destination, and I was about to be involved in an accident."

The cab driver twisted the steering wheel to the left then to the right, turned on the stereo to full volume and banged on the horn in succession, pulled the gear to neutral and pressed the accelerator on and off. The car sounded like a fire engine, drowning the noise of the demonstrators.

He then pushed the gear to number one, and pressed on the accelerator again. The people in front of the car looked into the driver's eyes and decided that he meant business. He was not joking. His patience had worn out. He let the car tear into them like an angry rhinoceros. I will never forget the look I saw in their eyes, and maybe they will never forget the look they saw in my eyes too as they looked at the car delivering death to them, and as they dived for their lives. I closed my eyes. We were all going to die anyway. If they had chosen to die with their eyes open I had opted to die with mine closed. I felt myself propelled forward as I hit the partition between me and the driver. Then I was thrown back on my seat. I opened my eyes probably to take a final look at the world before I died. We entered the tunnel at supersonic speed. At the speed we were careering through the tunnel, we were going to run into the car ahead of us and probably set up a chain reaction that would push all the cars ahead of us through to the other end of the tunnel. But the driver's instincts were to be trusted. He slowed down and soon we were cruising at an average speed of 50 m.p.h.

After recovering from the shock I sat back and thought over the events of my journey.

At 7 p.m. East African time, my driver Juma Mustafa drove the office car to my home. We had four hours before take off at the Dar es Salaam Airport. My cook had packed my two travelling bags, under Miriam's supervision. The executive bag where my papers and passport were kept in a special compartment was closed, and the keys were in my wallet together with the other keys for all my bags. We were ready for the drive to the airport.

Miriam had cancelled a date to watch a movie with her boyfriend in order to come and help me pack as well as escort me to the airport. I did not need to request her to come, because I knew she would have insisted on coming to the airport with me anyway. Besides, she claimed that she had already watched the whole movie at the drive-in cinema, some two years back. "But with a different boyfriend," I joked.

"Anyway, Nielsen is always here and you are going away so I better see you off. After all, I can even come to see him on my way from the airport," Miriam insisted.

Chief had insisted on coming to the airport to see me off in order to give me the last words of wisdom on how I was to conduct myself in U.S.A. But I managed to dissuade him from coming as the occasion would have been too official. I wanted to break off from the office formalities, as I was now a student. I no longer needed Chief around me to talk about the office. After all, he had understandingly said that I should go away from it all for a while.

Saying farewell to Juma my cook was an emotionally charged affair. We had shared very good times together and we had lived like one big and happy family. His wife wept openly. "We shall miss you, come back soon, study hard, run after the girls but do not marry them and come back to marry in Dar es Salaam," she advised.

"He is not going to America to marry, but to study," his daughter, Helen said.

I was thinking of how I would miss Mrs. Juma's favourite dish of half ripe bananas cooked in coconut milk mixed with groundnut stew. I told her so, to which she replied, "In United States they have the best food in the world, you will return as fat as a hippo, I guess."

Her daughter, Helen, insisted on leaving her homework to accompany me to the airport. Helen was at Shaban Robert Girls' Secondary School, and she used to come to the house sometimes when I was not working late or drinking at the New Africa Hotel or Oysterbay Hotel. I would help her with her homework. She was a bright girl, very good in mathematics. Her mother would not allow her to go anywhere else after school except to my house.

As we drove out of the compound in silence, I looked at my vacated Msasani Peninsula house, with lights off, bathed in moonlight and standing there with curtains drawn. I had certainly enjoyed myself in that house with the gorgeous kitchen, dining room, the living room with wonderful coaches, the two bedrooms for visitors, and the master bedroom, which Juma Mohammed kept so tidy and decorated like a nuptial room. I was wondering who would be allocated the house in my absence. Whoever he was he would certainly like it, but it did not matter. I would have an even better house when I got back. As Principal Secretary I would perhaps move into Chief's. I thought to myself.

As if reading my mind, Miriam said, "Do not mind about the house. You will not miss it. In U.S.A. you will live in a much better house."

"Sure," I said.

We drove down Msasani Road into Bagamoyo Road.
"We have lots of time," Miriam said, "Want a drink?"
"Sure," I answered. It seemed as if "sure" was the only word
I could utter.

At Salander bridge we were delayed a little. A pedestrian
had been knocked down by a landrover whose driver
seemed to have been drunk. The bleeding pedestrian was
being carried into a waiting ambulance as we drove by.

I then noticed that my driver was heading towards the
centre of the town because as soon as he heard of a drink he
headed to my favourite drinking place – the New Africa
Hotel.

I said, "Lets go to Palm Beach." I knew at New Africa
Hotel my friends would not let me go and that I would
probably miss the plane.

We parked at the Palm Beach parking lot, entered the
hotel and sat at a corner table. Soon, a waiter came to take
our orders. Two Safari beers, a coke and red wine. The wine
was for Miriam, the coke for Helen and beer for myself.
Miriam put in an order for roast goat ribs and spiced liver.

We had quite a party. The bar was full. As an Assistant
Principal Secretary, I could not sit in any bar in town without
friends recognizing me, but tonight nobody did because I sat
in the dim light, outside in the patio, in the company of two
females. The light below the coconut tree where we sat was
dim. The atmosphere was romantic. The fragrance of the
fruits and flowers of the cashewnut trees, the breeze from
the coconut trees and the moonlight superimposed with the
light from the blue bulbs, and the shadows of the coconut
leaves dancing on the ground, together with Helen and
Miriam on my side, created a romantic atmosphere which
you cannot find anywhere in the world, except at the coast
in the tropics.

"We have to go,"Miriam said at last. She was always in
charge. But soon I would be in charge of my own schedules.

We drove down Upanga Road into Samora Machel Avenue and Nkrumah Street. It was Miriam's idea that we drive across the city so that I could see it for the last time. It was now 10 p.m. and the streets were full of people coming out of bars, going to dance halls, movies or just standing, window shopping. Soon we were driving on Pugu Road and into the Dar es Salaam Airport.

At the airport, after I had checked in my luggage, Miriam insisted that we share another drink at the lounge where we sat looking at the Lufthansa airlines plane that had arrived earlier on from the Seychelles. This big bird would carry me from Dar es Salaam to London, and then on to Boston. Miriam, kept on giggling because she was very thrilled. We hugged and shook hands many times.

"Ladies and gentlemen, Lufthansa airlines flight 14BB is ready for boarding, will passengers prepare to walk to the plane please."

I had to go! Other passengers began to board. "I shall write."

"Send us pictures, work hard...."

We said so many things to each other. I had to leave before I was all worked up and exhausted. I left Helen and Miriam on the waving bay. They could watch the plane take off from there.

With the executive bag in my hand I mingled with the other passengers walking to the plane. Soon I heard from the balcony, "Bye, Fred!"

I shouted back, "Bye, Miriam, bye, Helen".

I wondered how from the waving bay they could figure me out in the crowd. Perhaps my new blue suit was conspicuous in the dim airport light? As I climbed the steps into the airplane I heard a final "There he is, bye, Fred". As I stood on the steps and waved, I could see Miriam quite well in the crowd on the balcony.

"Welcome aboard," the air hostess said. "Welcome to U.S.A.," I added mentally.

After a brief stop over in Cairo we proceeded to Frankfurt where we were delayed for two hours. There was a bomb scare at the airport and therefore airplanes, baggage and passengers were being thoroughly checked. There were armed security men all over the place. A terrorist group had vowed to bring down or bomb any German aircraft, I learnt.

Finally we took off, but in darkness. The take off was not even announced. I suppose this made the terrorists unable to know where or when to strike, but all the same I felt so vulnerable. I thought that in the dark the blinking lights from the aeroplane could be seen better and so it was easy to strike, but I trusted the security people. They knew better. I prayed that we do not crush down in a ball of fire over the airport, before I made it to the land of unlimited happiness.

Meanwhile, all went well and here I was, now being driven through the streets of Boston heading for the YMCA, where I would be staying for sometime before I got a permanent residence. We were now out of the tunnel and driving past supermarkets, streets flanked by tall buildings on both sides, and beautiful green parks that at this hour seemed empty.

A few more minutes of driving brought us to 655 Massachusetts Avenue – the YMCA. The fare meter read $11.

"Here you are brother, the Y is right here."

We had not spoken since we ran through that ordeal at the tunnel. I paid him $12. You always give a tip, it is an international custom. Anywhere you go in the world you find it.

"Hey! where are you from?"

"Tanzania," I said as I was getting out of the taxi.

"That is in the Caribbean, right?"

"No, it is in Africa, East Africa." I was glad to be educative.

Always teach some geography free of charge wherever you go. After all, you learn a lot and nobody charges you for it. Just like this driver trying to tell me that the cab driver at the airport refused to take me because I was black. This was free information!

"Welcome to Boston," the cab driver shouted as he drove off.

"Sure." I must stop answering in monosyllables. I thought it was not polite but the occasion did not demand any over extension of courtesy. Not after that incident at the airport and at the entrance into the tunnel.

The old lady at the YMCA front desk looked at me. I must have arrived at the wrong time because she was concentrating on her crossword puzzle which she had seemingly worked to about seventy five percent as far as I could see.

"Can I help you?"

"Do you have a room for me"

"Did you book?"

"Yes, my name is Fred Munyao, the World Bank rang, I hope to stay here for a while."

She ran her fingers through a list of names, looked at me through her gold rimmed spectacles then went to the rack for the keys.

"Upstairs room 325." She handed me the keys, her eyes on the crossword puzzle.

"Thank you." I said.

"Sure," she answered already writing another solution to her crossword puzzle. They become very easy if you are sixty five years as she probably was, and you perhaps did them since you knew how to spell.

My room at the YMCA was nice. In fact it was as good as the YMCA rooms in Dar es Salaam and Moshi where I used to stay whenever we went on a field project when I was a student. I was so impressed by the rooms at the YMCA in Dar es Salaam and Moshi so much so that on my first visit to Europe I stayed at a YMCA hostel. It was an old dirty place, I must say. Students liked it because it was cheap and affordable but it was not that clean and the food was awful. Always consisting of greasy fish and chips as if this was the only dish mankind had known since he discovered how to cook. I would not have survived another day in that hostel without coming down with a fatal bug. I moved out to a hotel the next day with a notion that not all YMCA hostels were good. The YMCA hostels can be bad, but of course this one had to be good being in America . . .

Everything here is beautiful, Chief had told me!

41

Chapter 4

Looking for an Apartment

I enquired from the lady at the reception of YMCA on how I could go about looking for an apartment. I needed a place to live in. A place of my own. The lady was working on one of those crossword puzzles again. She told me casually, "Today being a Sunday, look at the *Sunday Globe*. It runs hundreds of advertisements on vacant apartments."

I went out, bought the *Sunday Globe* and ran through the 'apartments to rent' pages trying to look for what the U.S.A. 1949 Housing Act referred to as a safe, decent and sanitary dwelling. However, the Act forgot to mention that you stood a better chance of getting a house if you have a combination of certain qualities: white, single, rich and male. If you are black, married, poor or female your chances are considerably curtailed. If you are married and with kids your chances are worse than if you were married and without kids.

"Apartment in a family house in Brooklyn, fit for a single student. Going $150 per month, ring 624-6582."

I quickly rang the number: "Hello, is that 624-6582?"

"Yes, what do you want?" a lady's voice answered.

"I am calling about your advertisement in today's paper . . . "

The lady did not let me finish. She cut me short with, "I am sorry, this is a white neighbourhood and we intend to keep it so. Are you a new person in town?"

"Yes," I answered shocked out of my skin. I wondered how she knew that I was black something that I myself had never thought about. I had never, and was not used to thinking of myself as a black man. I thought of myself as an Assistant Principal Secretary and not a black or white or blue man for that matter.

"Blacks live in Roxbury, Dorchester, Mattapan or Jamai-

42

can Plains." She slammed down the receiver. I nodded to myself, I have made two other discoveries. I am a black man and you can tell a black man by speaking to him on the phone. There are black and white neighbourhoods.

Another advertisement read, "A studio in the Back Bay going at $130 a month. To share bathroom with a student."

Again a female voice answered but this time it was a sweet and young voice. "Are you a student?" She asked.

"Yes. I will be going to Massachusetts School of Economics," I said.

"You are welcome to take the studio but as the advertisement said, the studio is adjoining mine and we will have to share the bathroom. I hope you do not mind sharing a bathroom with a lady. I do not mind sharing a bathroom with a man myself."

I was almost tempted to take the apartment only that I mentally pictured the situation I was getting into, soap bars and hair strings in the bathroom. We would have to use the bathroom in turns in the morning, and I imagined either of us standing outside the bathroom waiting for the other to finish whatever he or she was doing inside. For me it would be an embarrassing situation. I wished Miriam, my secretary was here to advise me. She would usually know how to handle this type of situation well.

I said to the lady, "I will give it a thought and call again" "Hurry," she said, "Apartments are scarce in Boston and this being an educational city, at this time of the year it is invaded by hundreds of students looking for apartments."

"I will try and hurry. Thank you, bye."

"Bye," She said rather sweetly.

The next advertisement that caught my eyes was, "A studio and one bedroom apartment on Huntington Avenue." I called and this time a man's voice answered. I explained that I was a student going to Massachusetts College of Economics. I had already learnt that the mere mention of Massachusetts

College of Economics due to its fame puts one several points on the positive side.

"Are you from Africa?"

I was being interviewed on the phone. "Yes, from Tanzania." I wanted to add that I was an Assistant Principal Secretary in the Ministry of National Economy, but I thought perhaps he was not familiar with these British derived titles.

"Where about is that? Is it near Nigeria?"

"No, it is in East Africa, in between Mozambique and Kenya," I said, trying not to sound like a geography teacher.

"Oh yes, I think I know where that is. Come and see what I have got for you. I have a very nice one bedroomed apartment and a studio. No rats, no cockroaches, no broken flooring and plumbing, peeling plaster and all that junk. You will be lucky to have one of these two vacancies. Come over tomorrow and look at them." He was a good telephone salesman. I told him that I would go over the following day. I hung up satisfied that I would take either the studio or the one bedroom apartment.

I left the YMCA building and walked into the cool autumn afternoon. On Massachussets Avenue cars were zooming to and fro. The sidewalks were full of shoppers, and possibly shoplifters, in colourful attire. I walked down the street and came to the train station. A man stood there all by himself.

"Is this where the train that goes into Boston stops?" I asked him politely.

"You are going to Roxbury?"

"No, I am going to Boston," I answered.

Then we stood quietly, two strangers having nothing to say to each other. A girl passed us swinging away, apparently not very mean about how much of her anatomy she revealed to the outside world.

"Some chick." The guy came to life. With some people

44

it takes nothing less than a girl to make them tick. "Oh boy, that girl is beautiful, ooh! the eyes, the butt, the hair, the way she walks – that was a wonderful work of art, whoever designed it!"

I was in no mood for a sermon about women. My major preoccupation was to go look for an apartment. I could not imagine staying for another day in a single room at the YMCA. I was already missing my Msasani Peninsula home.

"Beauty is in the eyes of the beholder," I said hoping that he would consider the topic closed.

"Coming from a black man that sounds very philosophical, you sound like the most intelligent blackman I have ever come across," he said smiling sardonically.

"Black," I noted mentally, and as I had nothing else to philosophize I kept quiet and looked up the street hoping that the train would show up soon. However the train did not come, instead a man carrying two framed pictures of Isaack Hayes walked down the street and stopped at my side. I was standing arms akimbo. He also stood arms akimbo with his left elbow touching my right elbow.

"Look," he said, gazing at both our arms. "Look, we are brothers, black brothers. Right?"

"Yeah," I said disinterestedly.

"Where are you going?"

"To Boston," I answered. "I am waiting for the train."

"Oh! brother, why don't you walk?"

"I guess it is a bit too far to walk, isn't it?" I was getting impatient.

"You are strong," he insisted, "Look at your tummy, you are a bit on the fat side."

I wanted to tell him, "What do you think of an Assistant Principal Secretary?"

"You could walk and lose some weight. You see, we black people are beautiful, very beautiful, we must not

45

become fat and ugly like the white people, so walk brother," he was literally ordering me.

Now I was fed up, really fed up. I was not fed up with my "brother", but fed up with the black and white talk. I repeated mentally, "black, white," and counted the number of times I had heard the two words in the last 18 hours I had been in the country. Since I arrived here the two words had been as if they were the only words in the English language.

I wondered quietly to myself. "Why is everybody talking black and white? Isn't there anything else to talk about? Is the city, the country or the whole world for that matter either black or white? Maybe this should be my first lesson even before I start studying for my Master's Degree in Economics. The world is either black or white. How about green, yellow, red, blue? It does not make sense, at least not to me. . ."

The guy broke my trend of thought with *"Wasalaam Aleikum,"* and briskly walked away. Not withstanding the fact that *"Aleikum Wasalaam"* is said when you meet and not when you part. I noted, "Well here they say *"Wasalaam Aleikum"* when they part and not when they meet, and believe that the world is either black or white. Back home we say *"Wasalaam Aleikum"*, when we meet and do not classify people according to their colour."

On the opposite side of the street two people were waddling down the street, one was black and the other was white. I decided to classify people into black and white too, because after all when you are in Rome, act as the Romans do. Both were fat so I decided fatness was not a distinguishing feature between blacks and whites.

I arrived at 2000B Huntington Avenue and rang the buildings' superintendent bell. Nobody appeared. I pressed the bell for the second time and waited patiently for about one minute. A young girl in a silk night gown opened the main gate into the premises. She looked sleepy and tired.

Her eyelids were drooped like she had *"Myasthenia Gravis"*. She could hardly open the gate.

"What do you want?" she challenged me in slurred speech.

"I am looking for the superintendent. Know where I can find him?" I asked.

"He is not up yet, come back in three hours time." She disappeared without another word.

"Well," I thought, "It is now 9 a.m. and therefore he was going to wake up at noon. He sure sleeps good. Supposing there was a fire in the building, would he be able to wake up to help the tenants?"

I stood in the lobby wondering what to do next. The postman arrived, threw his bag on the tiled floor, opened the mailboxes on the wall one by one, and started throwing letters into them while lazily humming a song. He looked bored and disgusted with his job.

"This place has so many tenants and so many mailboxes. It is just like a jail," he remarked without looking at me. He then turned to me. "I have not seen you around here, are you looking for an apartment here? To tell you the truth I would prefer the 'Watham House of Correction' to this place." "Besides, this is predominantly a white neighbourhood."

I did not care what he said, not even about his last comment. I was not listening to him. I needed an apartment for school was starting soon.

At noon, I came back to see the building superintendent. A middle aged man with a four day's growth of beard and protruding eyes opened the gate. He looked sleepy.

I had thought the girl I saw was his daughter, but now I changed my mind. The girl was his lover. Both of them were on drugs. They must have got pretty "high" but she managed to get out of the trance earlier than he did. I am told that women metabolize drugs faster than men. Something to do with their hormonal system. Also young people metabolize drugs much faster than old people. She was about eighteen and he was about forty-five.

The superintendent showed me a studio on the first floor and a one bedroom apartment on the second floor, both of them facing Huntington Avenue. As he drew the curtains and opened a window the rattling sound of the train came to my ears.

The one bedroom apartment looked OK. But it would cost me three hundred dollars per month. The studio had its paint peeling off at some places on the walls and it would cost me two hundred dollars per month. I looked the studio over. In the closet I found a lady's handbag, a packet of unused condoms and a box of tampax. I concluded that the former tenant must have been a female student, perhaps attending the nearby North Eastern University and that she was a very sociable girl.

Though I was an Assistant Principal Secretary I was going to live on a student stipend of five hundred dollars per month, and on this I could not afford a three hundred dollars per month apartment. So I decided to take the studio.

"If you like the studio, go to the Real Estate manager on 1800A Massachusetts Avenue and talk it over with him. He will need you to pay two months rent and a security deposit of two hundred dollars. I shall ring him up to say that you are going to see him."

Unfortunately, I did not know that 1800A Massachusetts Avenue was in Cambridge situated on the other side of Charles River, and not in Boston. So I went to 1800B in Boston. The Real Estate manager Mr. Perry Watts did not live there. I asked a fellow I found repairing a 1974 Valiant in front of 1800B Massachusetts Avenue, where I could find Mr. Perry Watts on 1800A Massachusetts Avenue. It seemed his old car required all the attention he could afford and he had none to spare for me. He said without looking at me,

"Why don't you look in the yellow pages, telephone him and he will tell you where to find him."

I telephoned Mr. Perry Watts. He told me to try and go to the office immediately, as he was leaving in an hour's time to attend to other business. I got on the MBTA bus, went up Massachusetts Avenue, crossed the Charles River, passed Massachusetts Institute of Technology (MIT) and there on my right was 1800A Massachusetts Avenue. As I walked in, I heard Mr. Watts giving instructions to his secretary, "A black man from Africa will be coming to see me. Tell him that I will see him tomorrow morning at ten and that he should come with the money, $600 if he wants the studio."

"Why did he have to be all that specific?" I thought to myself. "A black man not a white man, from Africa and not from America."

The former Assistant Principal Secretary was no longer referred to reverently as Mzee or Fred Munyao. He was now simply referred to as "a black man from Africa." He could have at least addressed me as a gentleman from Africa, but well, he was very specific. *A black man from Africa.*

As soon as he finished talking he looked over his shoulder and saw me. He did not even mind my hearing him referring to me simply as a black man from Africa. It was seemingly normal to refer to people that way, so he walked to me and said, "You must be the person who called. I am sorry I am going out, but my secretary will talk to you."

The secretary told me, "You go and look at the place, if you like it, come over tomorrow, pay one month's rent, security deposit of $200 and an extra one month's rent in case during the last month you decide to leave without paying."

"You think I will run away on the last month without paying your rent?" I asked her, surprised that I, a responsible Assistant Principal Secretary was not trusted.

"Some people do that, you know," she answered . "You

have to pay in cash, we do not accept cheques from strangers. Of course, you can subsequently pay by cheque, but we want cash, initially."

I had only $400 in my wallet, and I knew that I had no way of coming up with the extra two hundred before the following day, but it wouldn't be of any help explaining that to her.

"OK, I will come back tomorrow with the money," I told her.

"Good bye," she answered with her eyes on the electric typewriter.

It seemed to me that Mr. Watts and the secretary knew that I did not have the money and in fact they were hoping that I would fail to take up the apartment so that they would rent it to somebody else, probably a white person. I was determined to take it but did not know where to get the money from. I wished I had the money to surprise them with! The postman had asked me what I was doing looking for an apartment in a white neighbourhood. It seemed the landlord wanted to keep me out of the neighbourhood, but he did not want to tell me directly that he was not going to rent the apartment to a black man.

I was now determined to take the apartment. It will cost $200 a month, expensive, but it seemed to me that in America apartments were expensive be it in a black, white or yellow neighbourhood. I was determined to spend all the money I had, provided I got the studio, even if it meant living on bread and water until my next stipend came in.

While on the bus returning to the YMCA I sat quietly, deep in thought thinking of how I could come up with the extra $200. Suddenly an idea struck my mind. I said almost loudly, "I got it," and snapped my fingers. The lady seated next to me looked at me in amazement. I am sure she was thinking, "Just another mad black man." She was not aware that I was thinking of the Merylyn Jones Emergency Fund.

Anyway, it was not her business. Perhaps she had not been to college, and even if she did, she did not go to Massachusetts College of Economics. And even if she had been there, such a fund might not have existed during her time.

Merylyn Jones was a female student who came to Massachusetts College of Economics ten years ago, paid all the seven years' tuition fee in advance to do a Master's Degree and a Ph.D in Economics, only to die in a motor accident along Brooklyn Avenue a week after she had registered. She was a foreign student from France, and she had worked and saved for years to come to U.S.A. to study at the famous college of economics.

Along with the joining instructions which I had given to Miriam to read and summarize for me, there was the information about Merylyn Jones Emergency Fund. Miriam mentioned it to me but added, "Of course you will not need to borrow money in U.S.A. But in case you need to, the information in the joining instructions is that this girl's tuition fee was put in what is now called Merylyn Jones Emergency Fund, from which students could borrow money when they were in acute financial difficulty, provided they were trustworthy and they could return the money in three months time. One can borrow from this fund upto $600."

That is what I did. I borrowed six hundred dollars to enable me pay the deposit for my apartment in a white neighbourhood!

The next day I went to Mr. Watt's office to pay the six hundred dollars deposit. The secretary was surprised to see me back. She had seemingly thought that I would not come back. Before she could open her mouth to speak I placed the money in new one hundred dollar bills on her typing desk. I thought she was going to come up with excuses like, "Mr. Watts said he does not rent apartments to students, he is sorry the place burnt down last night, or

51

the apartment has been rented." But she went ahead and filled the lease forms and after five minutes, I walked out of her office with the lease forms signed and stamped.

Back at 2000B Huntington Avenue, I buzzed the superintendent. At first nobody answered. I buzzed again with my ear glued to the loudspeaker on the wall in the lobby hoping to hear, "Who is there?" Instead the main gate opened and the young girl appeared and opened the main gate. She wore a pair of designer jeans and a jordan marsh blouse that left three quarters of her large breasts exposed. Her hair was tied behind her head in two knots. Her eyes were wide open, revealing large dilated pupils. A trembling hand opened the door and through a trembling mouth came, "You do not have to buzz ten times, I am not deaf you know."

"Well, excuse me I am looking for the superintendent," I said with the politeness of a schoolboy hoping that her anger would cool down.

"Well, you are talking to the building superintendent, or whom do you think you are talking to?"

I thought, yesterday she had taken a sedating drug, today she had taken an excitory drug. Some drugs cause excitement and irritability while others cause sleepiness. But sometimes it was difficult to know what drugs one had taken, for excitement can also occur when one is recovering from a sedating drug. I could not tell what drug she had taken, excitory or sedative, but that was not my business.

She was about to close the door but fortunately for me, she saw the pink papers in my hand and recognized them as the lease forms from Mr. Watts' office. She went to call the superintendent and I heard her say to him, "A black tenant to see you. I think Mr. Watts has forgotten that this is a white neighbourhood and the Irish community wishes to keep it that way."

Mr. Georges, the superintendent appeared almost immediately. He was sleepy, presumably from the drug he had taken or perhaps he was recovering from an excitory one. Despite his condition he tried his best to help. In contrast with his girlfriend, he was very nice. He had to be nice, otherwise tenants would complain to Mr. Watts who would sack him. If he were to be sacked, he would lose his source of money to buy drugs for himself and his girlfriend. Without providing his girlfriend with the drugs she was addicted to, he would definitely lose her to another man.

Mr. Georges gave me the keys to the studio apartment and said, "You are now the legal owner of the studio for a period of one year."

Chapter 5

Back To School

The first week at school was a busy one, orientation, choosing courses and being introduced to academic advisors and course lecturers. When the weekend arrived, I was glad to forget about school. I spent the day shopping downtown and came back in the afternoon for a meal and a siesta. In the evening I thought I would look for a bar in the neighbourhood and take a beer. I walked up Huntington Avenue, came to Park Drive and wandered into a side street, Queensberry Street. I looked around. The sign caught my eye. "McNasty's for Beer and Music."

As I walked through the door a man with a wide sombrero appeared from nowhere and challenged me, "Two dollars cover." I fumbled into my pocket and handed a five dollar bill to him.

McNasty's was quite a place, there was music and lots of people. All white people; drinking, smoking and dancing.

I sat at the counter and ordered for a Budwiser and began to feel at home with the crowd. I had completely forgotten my loneliness, despite the fact that I had only one beer for company. A young man joined me at the counter. We got into talking. He worked at the Sheraton Hotel as a cashier and he was on his evening off.

Later he said, "Do you realise that you are the only black man here?"

I told him, "No I didn't, am I black?"

He looked surprised by the question so I went on to explain, "You see where I come from, we do not talk about people's colour. We do not care if you are black, white or blue."

"Here we do," he went on to say. "You'll later realise that there are certain places you'd rather not go to. Places where

54

people would not talk to you as cordially as I am doing now."

"I really would not care if people did not talk to me," I remarked.

"But no girl would talk to you in a singles' bar, like here at McNasty's except in downtown or Cambridge where there are singles' bars, where blacks and whites mix. Do you like singles' bars?" he asked.

"What are singles' bars?" I asked, having not heard the phrase before.

"Singles' bars are the kind where single men and women meet to drink, have a nice time, and make friends," he explained.

Looking around I discovered my environment, as if I was not aware of it all this time – the disco music, boys and girls seated, standing, dancing or talking romantically. So this was a singles' bar where boys and girls, men and women come to have fun. Men come here to pick women and women to pick men? Wasn't there a song about single bars? I continued to think to myself.

I could not remember the words of the song very well but I thought it did not matter.

The band played some sexy song and young people in jeans took to the floor, dancing exotically. In fact everything was exotic in this bar. A girl was presumably kissing a man who looked like her boyfriend at one corner of the bar, and a couple was necking while dancing on the floor. Here and there boys and girls, men and women were drinking and loving. Love was in the air!

I felt a bit lonely when the boy left me at the counter to join some two girls who had just walked in. I finished my beer and said to myself, "What is an Assistant Principal Secretary doing in this place of ill-repute?" I then walked out quietly.

The man with the sombrero was at the door to bid me "Goodnight, I hope you enjoyed yourself."

I said, "I sure did," and walked briskly into the cold evening. I walked down the street and retraced the way back to my studio apartment. I had left a piece of turkey in the fridge. I warmed it and ate it with some bread and retired to a good night's sleep. Thanks to the four *Budwisers* I had drank at McNasty's.

The next day was Sunday. I thought of going to church, any church and pray. In Dar es Salaam, I had developed the habit of going to any church provided there was a cross on top of the building. I would often pray at the church I happened to be near to, or any church my friends would take me to when I happened to be travelling upcountry in the districts. I never minded whether it was Lutheran, Catholic, Seventh Day Adventist, Anglican, whatever. Sometimes I would pray at Saint Peter's Church on Bagamoyo Road or at the Anglican Church on Upanga Road. I have even prayed at the Pentecostal Church in Temeke and some friends had even taken me to a Salvation Army religious meeting where I sang my heart out!

On this particular day in Boston I did not walk for long before I came to a church. Churches in Boston are in plenty, but church goers are very few. The first church I came to as I realised later when inside, was a Russian Methodist Church. I had not even bothered to read the name of the church on the large board outside. I just saw a large cross on the building and lots of cars parked outside and I walked in, knelt down and began to follow the Sunday service.

A young, fat, short priest was saying mass. I liked the vestments, the originality of the mass, whatever that means and the fact that the priest said mass facing away from us, and in a language that I did not understand. Having grown up before Vatican II, when the Catholic Church changed the mass to look as much as the last supper Christ shared with his disciples two centuries back, I liked masses said with the priest facing that way, in Latin, Greek or in Russian.

Soon I came to realise that people were staring at me. I looked around and realised that just like in the singles' bar I was the only black man around. But unlike in the single's bar where I left early, I was intending to stay here until the end of the service. I was very comfortable despite the stares until the time of giving alms. Back home the time of giving alms at church is a singing and joyous time. They sing a song that encourages people to give back freely to the Lord whatever He has given them. It said, "If the Lord has kept you safe and free of bad omen during the week, why can't you give back to him a little of what He gave to you?" Here in Boston, an old man goes around quietly with what looks like a small basket collecting alms. When he came to the place where I was kneeling and praying quietly like everybody else, he skipped me although I had my hand stretched out with one dollar bill in it.

Perhaps I should not have gone to that church. Just imagine an African man praying in a Russian church in U.S.A! I am sure they had something to talk about when they got home. "Tell you what, we had a black man in church today." But it was not my mistake. I did not know that blacks and whites pray in different churches. Even in Plain-Georgia where former President Jimmy Carter comes from, blacks and whites pray separately. They have these two churches standing side by side barely a hundred yards apart, blacks to this church and whites to the other. When the former President visited from Washington, being the President of both blacks and whites, he used to attend Sunday services in the two churches. He went first to the white's church, then to the black people's. During the next visit he would first attend at the black's then at the white's. When you are a President you must try to please everyone. I wondered what he was doing now that he no longer was

57

President. Does he attend mass at both churches? Perhaps not, he does not need to please everybody anymore. One church – the white's church would be sufficient. I am sure he looks back and says, "It was rather ridiculous attending mass in two churches on one Sunday. The funny things I used to do because of the Presidency!"

*   *   *

On Monday classes started. The Assistant Principal Secretary was now a student and no longer the government bureaucrat he used to be in Dar es Salaam. I soon got into the routine of attending lectures, doing homework and doing the day's readings in preparation for the following day's lectures. It was not easy to get into this routine because it was a long time since I was in school. I felt the pressure of work. Too many lectures, reading, discussion group sessions, homework and tests. However my problem was not related to academics. It was what you could refer to as a social problem. I felt lonely. The loneliness engulfed me whenever I returned home from school and during the weekends. In the school, I felt part of the crowd of two thousand students. But back at my studio apartment on 1850B Huntington Avenue, I felt cold and lonely.

My routine and life style changed completely. My Msasani four bedroom house was replaced by a one bedroom–cum–sitting room studio apartment, almost like the type that bachelors live in at Temeke or Magomeni, in Dar es Salaam. The top Executives, Ministers in government, General Managers and Ambassadors that I had for neighbours in Msasani Peninsula, were replaced by noisy low class neighbours. A drug addict lived upstairs, an old lady lived alone in the apartment next to mine and a homosexual pair lived across the hall. My black official Mercedes Benz with the GT (Government of Tanzania) number plates was replaced by the Boston commuter train–where I rode with the working class of Boston.

I missed my bedroom with the large twin beds covered with clean blue sheets that Mzee Juma Mohammed, my cook, used to change, every two days. The studio apartment was of course, nothing compared to my Msasani Peninsula four bedroom house. The studio consisted of a bedroom which also served as a sitting room, a bathroom and toilet and a tin size kitchen. I hated the sitting-cum-bedroom which also served as my study room as well as the dining room. But I hated the kitchen most. The only place I liked was the bathroom, unfortunately one cannot stay for long in the bathroom. You go in there, finish whatever you are to do and you come out immediately.

The office, the bar, the friends, the Msasani home – this was my idea of a balanced life, just like a balanced diet with ingredients like carbohydrates, proteins, fats, vitamins and minerals. This is what we used to learn in our biology classes – all mixed up in the right proportions, containing levels of carcinogens toxic substances, chemical bacteria or viruses. My life, by all means and purposes used to be a balanced one, but in Boston it was far from balanced. This was because with the ingredients I had at my disposal, it was impossible to prepare a recipe for a balanced life. The ingredients I had consisted of classes, homework, readings, a studio apartment and the train as my means of transportation. I was an innocent, soft spoken, top civil servant brutally plucked from a life of responsibility, privilege and socialising, and catapulted into an alien world where one is lonely, life is dull, and the so–called men of colour are looked down upon.

When you are lonely, when your spirits are down, you can always find refuge in a bar. This is what I used to do in Dar es Salaam. Company and good time were in plenty at the Police Officers Mess at Msasani Club, Oysterbay Hotel, the NDC Club or, if I happened to be in the centre of town – The New African Hotel.

So one day after school I decided to forget about the readings, homework and the studio apartment for a while and walked around the neighbourhood looking for a bar, hoping that I would not end up at McNasty's again.

I ended up at a place called Linwood Ale House, where I sat at the counter and ordered for a Budwiser. A young man joined me at the counter and ordered for a Miller Light. He looked at my bottle and commented, "You drink that?" He seemed to realise that I was not enjoying my Budwiser. Actually I drank Budwiser because it was the only brand of beer that I had ever tried to drink. "Next time try my brand, Miller Light. I have tried all the beers made in this country and finally settled on Miller Light."

So I changed to Miller Light. It was not a bad beer. We got into talking. We discussed how beer was made and the fact that it was not easy for some people to distinguish beer from ale. The conversation switched over from beer to more radical issues which demonstrated that he was a dissatisfied member of the society. He talked about how the oil companies were swindling the present administration. He said that the administration was being bribed by the oil and nuclear companies and instead of investing in solar energy, which was cheaper and safer, it paid millions of dollars to the oil companies to import oil. He talked about the dangers of plutonium, and how American scientists were dumping the residues of it in the Third World because they had no place to keep it safe in America. He talked about the fact that drivers in Boston were the roughest and most reckless in the whole of the United States and concluded that, "If you cannot beat them join them."

He talked about how he did not like South Africa and the way they were treating the blacks, working them to their graves while the white man enjoyed the fruits of their labour.

He went on to explain that he was born into an Irish family and grew up in an all Irish neighbourhood. In their family blacks were often referred to as "dirty niggers," he said. They believed that they smelled, were thieves, and could steal from a dying person. However, history tells us that the Irish were driven away from Europe by the Great Potato Famine that killed three quarters of the Irish people. A great portion of those who remained alive arrived dead or barely alive on the shores of U.S.A. They fought for jobs in the coal mines and the railways and worked side by side with blacks, but because they were white they were given better jobs like supervisors and store keepers. Because they were given preferential treatment they very soon got ahead of the blacks and they have been ahead of the blacks ever since. Believe it or not, they started out together with the blacks there in the ghettos!

Later, after downing several Miller Lights the young man revealed to me that he was a school dropout. One day his teacher, an Irish nun, abused him because he did not finish his homework and so he called her an obscene thing. My heart almost missed a beat when he pronounced the word he had used against her, because I was not used to obscene words. Neither was the nun, I guessed. Perhaps her heart must have missed several beats if that was what he called her. I understand that nuns are very sensitive to obscene words. I imagined her crossing herself or going for her holy rosary when she heard the word.

"And that is the last I ever saw of the inside of a school," he confessed. "I now work as an engineer at a motel in town where most of my friends are Spiks, Haitians and blacks."

By "engineer," I guessed he meant a sweeper. How could a primary school dropout be an engineer?

"What are spiks?" I asked.

"Portaricans," he answered,"It is a racial slur. This damn country is full of racial slurs. You see when a white man talks to them they answer, 'no spik English', so they call them spiks."

It was nice talking to this young school dropout. I did not care and feel bad about the Assistant Principal Secretary now attending a reputable college drinking and conversing with a school dropout. When I later mentioned to him that I was a student from Africa doing my Master's Degree at the Massachusetts College of Economics, he almost dropped his glass of beer in surprise. He called the barman, "Look who is here. We have a Massachusetts College of Economics student here tonight, and a black one too!"

The barman looked at me and said: "I cannot remember when we last had a man from MCE in here. Last week we had a Harvard man, he sat on the very stool you are sitting on. We shall be happy to have intellectuals coming in here more often. Man, you are lucky to go to that college. You must be very intelligent. In fact that school had a long tradition of not admitting black people. I am told the first time blacks walked into the campus and sat side by side with white students, the white students and their parents threatened to withdraw from the school. 'How can our sons and daughters go to school with black people?' They asked. It took the U.S. army to quell the riots that erupted at the school."

The conversation was getting too racial for my liking, and I had homework to do, so I bid the barman and the Irish school dropout goodnight and retired to my studio apartment.

Columbus Day came and we had a holiday to commemorate the day he set foot on the American soil. I had by this time made friends with one of the male students at the school. Having worked as a Peace Corp in Senegal and Asia he was used to foreigners and so he did not keep his distance from foreigners as most of the local students at the school did.

"Come to dinner at my house tomorrow. I am having an international group coming over. We shall have some fun," he said to me when we closed school on a Thursday in preparation for the long weekend.

I accepted my first invitation to a student's house. Back home Chief had stressed to me that people were very generous when it came to inviting foreigners to their homes.

We had a delicious dinner consisting of chicken with mixed salad and seasoned rice.

"Do you eat chicken in your country?" A young man asked me as I was chewing a chicken wing.

"Yes," I answered. As an after thought I added, "Of course we have some people who do not eat chicken especially old people, they prefer cow or goat meat to chicken. They think it is unbecoming eating meat from such a small animal like a bird. In fact my grandmother does not eat chicken!"

The table was quiet, too quiet for my liking. "Why doesn't somebody start some interesting conversation?" I thought. Later as I was helping myself to some more rice I thought, "Hell, here I am an APS discussing with an eighteen year old about whether or not we eat chicken in my country, instead of discussing some world issues like the Soviet's invasion of Afghanistan, the North-South dialogue, the I.M.F. or the presidential campaign. The issue of eating or not eating chicken was chicken feed compared to these issues," I thought quietly.

We went on to discuss about the school, the courses, the way they kept us busy all the time, lectures and homework. The conversation however, did not interest me for long because it soon got too racial. An American asked a student from the Orient, "Are you from Korea?"

"No," his friend answered emphatically, "I am from Japan. You know we Japanese do not like to be called Koreans."

"I am sorry," the American smiled.

The Japanese continued, "You see, we look down on the Koreans just like you whites look down on blacks."

I felt like rising and leaving quietly. I was fed up with all the talk about whites, blacks, Japanese, Koreans, chickens and all.

"Why doesn't somebody start an interesting conversation?" I asked myself again. I gave myself another helping of the fried chicken, bit into a chicken leg and remarked, "this is very nice chicken."

To which our host answered, "Thank you."

The Japanese student came in with, "Do you eat chicken in Africa?" I answered, "Umm . . ." and continued to chew on the chicken leg. I was not going to discuss chicken feed again!

On my way back I entered Winnies Bar in Arlington. I had had some wine during dinner, but I am not a wine man. I am essentially a beer man. I had decided to try something new, Michelob Beer. I liked Michelob Beer but still it was not as good and as strong as the Safari Beer. In Dodoma during those days when Tanzania was making several brands of beer, Safari Beer used to be called "the hammer." After drinking two Safaris you felt like you had been knocked on the head with a hammer, and after imbibing four, you would feel like there were workmen breaking stones in your head. But the good thing about Safari Beer was not its strength, it was its taste and odour. Its taste and odour were attributes of good beer. The Ndovu too, when it was available on the market, was good beer, and, in fact, at Hotel Skyway or Mawenzi, I would always ask for Ndovu. As I looked at the barman behind the counter in Arlington, I wished I could say, "Safari please, and if you do not have it, make it Ndovu please." However there was no other way, I had to settle for a Michelob.

There is something funny about bars. No two bars and or

barmen look alike. The barman here at Arlington wore a T-Shirt with "Kiss me I am Irish," written in green letters on it. Behind him was an old door that looked as if it had not been opened for a long time. Written on it in bold letters were the words, "Slave Quarters."

The bar had very few customers. I sat at the counter and looked around. People sat around talking, drinking and smoking. There were two ladies in black slacks and green blouses dancing and flirting with a bearded man. By the look of his overalls one could easily tell his occupation – a painter. From the jukebox poured, *another one bites the dust* and, the two ladies and the gentleman on the floor were swinging away. The ladies were planting kisses, in turns, on the gentleman's unshaven cheeks.

Seated all alone, I began to think of the Hotel Skyway Bar on Sokoine Drive in Dar es Salaam. I was a frequent customer at this bar and many customers knew me. "Hi! Fred, how is the world treating you?" Here and there friends would greet me and I would shout back greetings across the huge counter and to various corners of the bar. Beers would be placed before me. An offer from the gentleman seated with the Somali lady over there, an offer from Shem, an offer from Mr. Maganga. I would not even bother to say, "Tell them 'thank you,' " because buying drinks for each other was a normal thing at Hotel Skyway. We were friends and friends bought each other drinks. But here at Winnies bar in Arlington, Boston, everybody bought beer for himself. Nobody knew me and nobody bought me beer. I did not know anybody and I did not buy anybody a beer.

The girls dancing on the floor reminded me of how girls would walk the floor of the Hotel Skyway Bar. There were girls of all shapes and sizes. There were slim girls, fat girls, tall girls, short girls – there were girls of all kinds. There were Somali girls, local girls, old girls, young girls, all dressed up beautifully. Some in tight American jeans and blouses from Europe. In fact, thinking about it now, the Skyway Hotel Bar looked like a Tanzania version of a singles' bar.

The music had stopped and the gentleman who was dancing with the two ladies passed by me going to the bathroom. On his way back as he was passing by me again he said loudly enough for me to hear, 'We have a man from Roxbury here today."

I recapitulated mentally and wondered, "A black man must always be from Roxbury. He could not be from Mississippi, Georgia, Washington, Cambridge or from Africa, like I was. He must always come from that depressed part of Boston – Roxbury, but who cares ?

I sat in the bar for two hours and downed four beers. Every time my bottle showed signs of drying up the barman would come and say, "You want another one?" The other people seated on the counter would call for their beer when they felt like having another one. "Yes, please," they would call, but for me I was seemingly being given preferential treatment.

He would always ask me as if he wanted to say to me, "Here, drink, take your fill and go." But I kept on drinking and when he no longer asked me, "You want another one?" I left.

For the two hours I had sat in the bar the only words I had said were, "Yes, please," in response to the barman's "You want another one?" It was the longest time I had ever stayed in a bar all by myself. Back home I would always have company.

As I walked down Huntington Avenue, headed back to my lonely studio apartment, I thought to myself, "Back home I would not have walked from the bar. I would have got a lift from my friends or if I was at the Hotel Skyway the manager would have told the driver to take me home in the hotel limousine."

I seemed to be thinking a lot about home this evening. As I opened the door to my apartment I was thinking of how my cook, Mzee Juma, would have come from his living quarters, as soon as he heard me arrive at the door, to serve my dinner. This evening there was no Mzee Juma and, despite the fact that I had had a lot to eat at dinner, I was already hungry. With the chilly weather one feels hungry all the time. It is not like in Dar es Salaam where in the hot humid weather one feels thirsty all the time. Here in Boston, you feel hungry all the time. This evening I managed to put some kind of supper together. Not much of a supper anyway. I opened a can of tinned beans, fried an egg, and with a slice of bread and a glass of orange juice I convinced myself that I was having a fairly balanced meal.

Again Sunday came and I had to go to church. I seemed to be very much interested in going to church and yet back home I could miss church even for four consecutive Sundays.

During my evening walks I had passed by a beautiful little church in the compound of a Parochial school. This is where I decided to go and pray this Sunday. Being a catholic, I thought I had better stop venturing into other people's churches, under the pretence of unifying all the christian churches under the same Christ, and start attending mass only at catholic churches, as I used to do before I became a liberal christian.

At the gate into the church I was confronted by a security guard. He wore a pistol on his hip, "If you want to pray here first talk to Father James over there."

I kept cool and thought it was funny posting a pistol totting security guard at the door of a church to keep away intruders. After all, Christ with his outstretched arms had said, "All men come to me," and here I was, going to Christ only to be stopped by a security guard!

Father James was putting on his vestments and at the

same time he was watching us. He must have seen the look on my face and knew what I was thinking. "Back home priests ask us to go to church, but here you must ask for permission from a priest to attend mass."

He walked over to me and said, "It is alright, we always have visitors come in to pray with us on Sundays, you are very welcome."

*　　　*　　　*

The second week of lectures, with the usual homework and reading was yet another very lonely week. I don't know why, but one never gets used to loneliness. Loneliness would engulf me as soon as I opened the door and got into the cold and lonesome interior of my apartment. I would put together a meal, eat alone, read, watch TV and go to bed only to wake up the next day to another boring routine consisting of school, house chores, meals, reading, television, sleep.

It is true that I was lonely only when I arrived home. I was lonely even on the train when going to, or coming home from school. It is funny that I never felt lonely sitting alone at the back of my office Mercedes Benz, being driven home from work, but on the subway train in Boston I often felt lonely despite the crowd around me. A lonely man should feel relieved when he gets into a crowded train, but even on the train, while mingling among the working class of Boston, one can feel lonely. Soon, one notices that when a black person takes a seat nobody comes to sit beside him, unless that person is also black or unless there is no other seat available. Even when there is no other vacant seat you see a white person standing while besides him there is a vacant seat. He or she will not take it because they will have to share it with a black person. You see a look of revulsion on a white person's face when he or she shares a seat with a black passenger. Some will look the other way or, if possible, sit with their backs to the black passenger on the same seat.

I asked the black passenger sharing a seat with me, "Why do white people avoid sharing a seat with a black person? Do the black people in this country suffer from a deadly disease like plague?"

"You talk about sharing seats on the train?" he asked, "You should have seen the humiliation of the blacks before the Civil Rights movement of the 60's."

He went on to explain at length how before the Civil Rights movement, blacks were denied the vote, they were segregated, had their own schools, bars and restaurants. Blacks were not allowed into facilities used by the whites. But it was difficult to arrange for separate transport facilities for the blacks and whites so the buses had two doors. Whites entered by the front door and occupied the front seats while blacks entered through the back door and sat at the back of the bus.

I wondered what happened when the black seats were full and some of the white seats were free. He explained that when all the black seats had been occupied the driver would not open the back door for more blacks to come in. He would only open the front door to let in whites or he would open the back door to let in blacks, but they would have to stand at the back of the bus even if there were empty seats in front. It was the same for the whites. If the white seats were full, whites would not occupy the black seats. They would rather stand crowded at the whites part of the bus rather than sit with the blacks.

My black seatmate on the train thought that blacks had come a long way, and I should not be concerned about whites who now refuse to share train seats with blacks.

Once you leave the train you think that is the end of the racial atmosphere but, in Boston, the racial atmosphere is always with you. It hits you from left and right.

From the train I used to come home and lie on the bed to relax with the evening paper. Most of the first page as usual is full of the news of the time, like the Iranian hostage crisis, or rather, the American hostages in Iran. A group of Iranian youths were taking hostage the whole of the American embassy staff in Teheran and the world was eagerly waiting for another Entebbe–like hostage operation to be mounted by the most powerful nation in the world. But America chose to play it diplomatically to avoid loss of lives. Some people thought America was showing too much patience. "U.S.A. should go in and rescue its citizens. Why is the most powerful nation on earth not doing so?" they asked.

One person in the name of Moshe Dayan had written in the evening paper, "The American army cannot rescue its citizens because it is a weak army and it is weak because it is composed of too many blacks up to sergeant level, and blacks are not educated and intelligent enough."

Racial news in the papers continue to hit you from left to right. *"Two white people booked for murder,"* says a headline. They had gone out to hunt deer, and having been at it the whole day, and not finding a single one they decided to return home. On their way home they saw a cow. One of them said to his mate, "Let's shoot the cow." The guy shot and missed. Later they came across a black man. Again the man told his mate, "Let's at least kill something today, how about him?" He raised his gun, aimed and fired. The man fell on his back. "Good shot," his mate remarked smiling and satisfied.

"There is a killer of black people around," says yet another headline. "He likes to kill black people in white female company. He killed two black men he saw jogging with white girls, and a blackman he found kissing a white girl in a park . . . ."

"In Atlanta Georgia they had counted eleven dead black kids in a period of one month. Almost every week, two black kids are pulled out dead from a river. It is suspected that a

70

white man, who hates the black race is responsible for these murders . . . ."

Soon you get tired of reading the paper and you start reading your notes. After all, you did not come all the way from Africa to read racial nonsense. But soon you are tired of reading. You cannot read academic books for a long time because it is a long while since you were in school, so you turn on the TV. Archie Bunker is on. Archie is a widower living with his niece and a black house maid (on TV housemaids and chauffeurs are always black). Archie goes to the supermarket with his housemaid. They are going around the shelves putting this and that into their shopping cart. People in the supermarket look and stare at them, a white person accompanied by a black female. They all look surprised. Even the cashier stops whatever he is doing at the cash register to stare at Archie. A long queue forms at the cashier's desk and almost everybody in the store is staring at Archie, and they believe that she is his wife. They are not used to seeing a white man married to a black woman and vice versa. A black-white couple is unusual in America, and people, especially whites, are discouraged by their families and community from entering into such unions. If one dares enter into such a matrimony, they will be sneered at by their colleagues. And that is what happened to Archie when he joined the queue with his presumed black wife, to pay for his groceries.

People began to whisper, "A Nigger lover."
Archie took it coolly but when he arrived at the cashier's desk he was boiling with anger and rage. The register clerk asked him casually, "Are you a Nigger lover?"

Archie threw a fist at him but his housemaid restrained him and said, "Don't worry, fellows. I am not his wife, I am his housemaid." But this did not stop the whispers!

A fat white lady says to her husband, "Why does he come

71

shopping with his housemaid? Why not give her the money so she does the shopping herself?"

The husband says, "You cannot trust black people, they can even fake receipts when they return the change."

Archie tries to throw his fist again at the clerk as he walks out of the store with his housemaid carrying the groceries. I then feel like throwing my fist at the TV screen but I don't. I turn to another channel.

On channel 25 they are showing that twice a week dancing competition – Dance Fever. Here blacks dance with blacks and whites with whites. They always draw a line across the two races even at social gatherings.

Finally you decide to continue reading your notes and try to make sense out of the day's lecture on the Du Pont Company, and the ways to stimulate production in the Company.

Later you go to the kitchen to prepare soup or coffee. You notice that the sink is full of three days' unwashed dishes and so you decide to do the dishes. I, an Assistant Principal Secretary washing dishes at 11 p.m. in a lonely studio apartment in the centre of Boston!

How do you start learning how to keep house at 35 years of age? House chores are for housewives, housemaids and houseboys. I, the former Assistant Principal Secretary, tidying up after meals, buying my own groceries and cooking, making my own bed, sweeping the floor, dusting, polishing, scrubbing, sluicing, doing laundry. I could not do it. Besides I did not even know where to start.

Soon the house became a mess. Nothing was in its right place. There was a member of a pair of socks under the bed while the other was in the toilet. Plates, forks, knives, cups and coffee mugs lay all over the place. Books, papers, shirts, and trousers lay here and there. A simple move from the bedroom to the toilet or from the bedroom to the kitchen would force you to pass over or walk on so many items, breaking some in the process.

While reading the paper one morning, I thought I had found the answer. In the land of the rich there is an answer to everything. The answer to my problem was a robot. They had discovered how to assemble a robot to do housework. The robot comes with a small computer. All that you have to do is to order it to do what you want by punching the computer keys. The robot will clean the house, sweep the floor, make the bed, put everything in its place, and return to sit at its place at the corner of the room to wait for more orders.

However, at the bottom of the page there was bad news for me. The robot cost forty thousand dollars. In the land of the rich there were things that only the very rich could afford.

Robot or not robot, I had to keep the house tidy so I decided to work out an organized system. First, I decided that everything must be put in its right place. Like the shirts must be in the closet, the socks in the middle drawer of my writing desk, and all dirty laundry would be thrown into a special paper box at the bottom of the bed. The crockery belonged to the kitchen where dirty dishes would be placed in the sink and clean ones in the drying rack or in the cupboard. It took a whole Saturday morning to get the place cleaned up and look habitable again. Now it looked more or less like a place where a former Assistant Principal Secretary could live, though not quite.

But it did not stay that way for long, because by the following Wednesday it was back to the same old mess. The sink was full of three days' dishes, the garbage pail in the kitchen was overflowing and smelling, and I had eaten from four plates and drank coffee from two mugs and two cups, that now lay unwashed in several parts of the studio. I made another resolution. I would spend about half an hour every morning before going to school or every evening after school cleaning up. I would wash all the dishes used the previous day, wash the cooking pots, sweep, take out the garbage, wash the bath and the toilet and sweep under the bed, where I would always find a member of a pair of socks or an underwear that had been lost. I decided that to survive I must not only go to school, but be a houseboy as well. I would have been alright if I was a full time houseboy, but to go to school and be a houseboy at the same time was no easy task. The house, though small, required a full time houseboy just like I had had in Dar es Salaam. Not one who was going to school and doing housework at the same time.

Chapter 6

Betty

It was a warm evening by Boston standards, considering that it was the month of October. I could not help going for a walk, a lonely one as usual. I walked down Park Drive, past Queensberry Street and up Malberry Street. The sidewalks were teeming with joggers, lovers and women dressed as sparsely as possible. There were women with backs exposed, necks exposed and thighs exposed so that you could see any part of the female anatomy you were particularly interested in. Despite my loneliness I was pleased to be alive. It was a very nice and happy day indeed and I was glad to be one in the crowd. I did not want my loneliness to weigh me down, so I walked down the street briskly, trying to be as happy as everybody else.

I did, however, get lonely again when I arrived in the public gardens in Arlington. The public gardens were rich with the bright colours of autumn. It was full of families, lovers and friends enjoying the sun. Here and there people played, ate, patted, touched, embraced, laughed, hugged and even kissed. It was a very happy atmosphere. A girl whose hips were held tightly by a pair of shorts that left a small lip of the lower end of her right buttock uncovered passed by me. She was passionately kissing her teenage boyfriend who seemed unconcerned. Two homosexuals, judging from their long hair, feminine complexion and the way they held hands, passed by, looking romantically into each other's eyes.

I decided that it was a very happy atmosphere for everybody, except me.

The atmosphere was too romantic, painfully romantic for a middle aged male with hot African blood racing in his veins. I had to leave the place before the blood that was racing into my head caused intra-cerebral bleeding. I walked down Arlington Street, down Boylston Street and into the subway.

The train was packed with commuters coming from work. They were packed in the train like sardines in a shopping basket. I could not get in, so I squeezed myself in at the steps near the door. A woman with a small dog shared the steps with me. Her Australian terrier kept on gnawing at my trousers and kept me wondering and waiting for the time it would bite my leg muscle. The train stopped at the Copley station to take on more of the working people while some got off. As I was standing at the stairs I had to squeeze in to make way for those alighting. This was not easy with my trouser's leg in the dog's mouth. I edged on one side to let those alighting go down the stairs before I could make my way into the train. The woman with the dog behind me did the same. A gentleman coming down the stairs comfortably through the clearing that we had made singled me out of the crowd, "Who do you think you are blocking the entrance? Either get in or get out!"

If I stayed for another minute on this train I would be suffocated. Fortunately I got off at Fenway Park. I walked slowly past Sears and across Brooklyn Avenue into the parking lot in front of Star Market. Suddenly, I heard the loud explosion of a tyre burst behind me. I stood on the sidewalk to see what had happened, then watched the traffic for a while.

Then I saw her. A young, slim woman standing on the opposite side of the street waiting to cross the street to where I was standing. She was as beautiful as the roses a high school student standing near her was trying to convince a motorist to buy. Although I had seen beautiful girls in this and other towns before, I was exceptionally captivated by her beauty.

There was something peculiar about her. I watched her

76

for thirty seconds or so and, as the traffic lights turned red and the traffic came to a stand still, she looked left and right and crossed, my eyes still on her. She was tall, about five and half feet. She was dark, smooth dark, that darkness that you do not only see but feel, with your eyes.

Her nose was peculiar. I felt I had seen that beauty in a nose before, but I could not remember where? The way her hair was tied in knots was also peculiar. I had not seen such a hair do for a long time, but I felt sure that I had seen it somewhere.

She wore a T-shirt plus or minus a bra. I could not exactly tell if she was wearing one. All that I could notice were thick teats bulging out of her thin chest. She wore a skirt, a blue one to match the colour of her small shoes and the T-shirt.

As she stopped on the sidewalk on my side of the road, she noticed me and I was caught unawares. She must have noticed that I was watching her, but I did not care. Men are always looking at women and women like being appreciated.

She passed without looking at me and went up Brooklyn Avenue, past the Macdonald parking lot into Arby's. There was something peculiar about the way she walked, the way she carried herself with her well formed legs, and the way she swung her hips below the skirt. In fact, there were so many interesting things about her that eventually, standing there all alone on the side walk, I decided in my heart that she was not American. Yeah! She was not American. She was African. But it did not matter. She could have come from any one of those fifty plus countries in Africa, even from South Africa or Namibia. But what business of mine was it? I decided.

As I walked into Star Market to buy groceries, I could not get her out of my mind. I considered myself silly to be thinking about a girl I had only seen in the street. She was, after all, one among the one hundred and ten million women

77

in America. Yes, she could be from Africa, so what? So was I. She could be from West Africa, perhaps Gabon, Nigeria, Ghana, Niger, wherever, and she could be somebody's wife.

"Thou shall not covet thy neighbour's wife," I reminded myself.

I decided to let her off my mind. After all, the chances of seeing her again were very slim. It was by chance really that she happened to be there, when I was there.

All the same she was African, I concluded. I knew it as soon as she entered my vision. I was quite certain she was from Africa. I should have talked to her. Oh! How nice it would have been to talk to somebody, let alone to talk to a person from Africa! To a beautiful lady too. It was a long time since I had chatted with an African lady or any lady for that matter. But then suppose she was not from Africa. Suppose she was an Afro-American from Roxbury, Dorchester or Mattapan?

"Hi!" I would have said.

"Hi!" she would have answered in a black American accent and, without even looking at me, she would have swung her hips away thinking, "Just another crazy heterosexual who thinks he can make a pass at any woman on the side walk."

As I started concentrating on the food shelves in Star Market I managed to get her out of my mind, completely.

I used to do my shopping every Friday evening. After school, I would go to Star Market on the Brooklyn Avenue opposite Sears. I had never bought groceries before in my lifetime. When I was a child, my food was either provided for by my mother, or by school cooks when I was in school, and by Mzee Juma, my cook, when I became an Assistant Principal Secretary in Dar es Salaam. With Mzee Juma , all I did was give him money and I would find food on the table. Sometimes I would bring the meat myself. I did not actually buy it myself. I would telephone Tanganyika Butchery on Uhuru Street and order for the meat, then I would send my driver to pick it up and take it to Mzee Juma. I liked buying my meat from Tanganyika Butchery because I knew the owner, and also a nephew of Mzee Juma worked there. Therefore, I was assured of the best goat ribs, ox liver, fillet, steak or even the best bones for my dog.

I had never carried a grocery bag in my lifetime, but in Boston I had to buy my own groceries, carry them home, cook my own food, eat alone and clean the dishes.

But as the saying goes, "Every cloud has a silver lining." I would not have met Betty, if I had not gone to buy groceries from Star Market.

One Friday evening after school, I went to Star Market as usual. I had made a shopping list consisting of chicken wings, pork chops, salads, bread, butter, Jamaican sugar, potatoes, red wine and a half dozen pack of Heinkein Beer.

As I was pushing my shopping trolley along the beverages' lane I saw her. She was reading the label on a can of food. I watched her for half a minute and went to the bread shelf. She picked up a bottle of candies and walked towards the back of the store to where the meats were. I watched her as she walked. She had well formed legs and hips. She was very beautiful. She had the longest neck I had ever seen. I decided that she was the same woman I had seen a week ago. I was determined to speak to her.

I saw her walk to the cash registers and I decided to cut my shopping list short. "I must stop buying groceries and talk to her, after all I can come to buy these groceries tomorrow, I quickly decided. I wheeled my trolley fast so that I was the next in the queue, behind her. I was acting like a teenager, now that I think about it.

The tellér took her groceries item by item. She had four items while I had eight. She asked the teller, while dipping her hand in her handbag, "How much are these, please?"

I gazed at her, trying to hide my surprise. She had an African accent, a rarity in Boston. I was charmed by her accent and I was wondering which part of Africa she could be coming from! Could she be from Kenya or Tanzania? I wondered to myself, perhaps I should say to her, *"Habari gani dada?"* to see if she understood Kiswahili.

I had feared that as the teller handled my groceries and by the time I was paying the bill, this beautiful girl would walk out of the store, and I would lose sight of her, but no. It happened that she had to leave her groceries at the teller's desk to go and cash a traveller's cheque at a nearby window before she could pay the bill.

As she was away to cash the bill, I was being attended to but I was not paying any attention. I was watching her. I was completely unaware of what was happening around me until the teller said, "Eight dollars and fifty cents please."

I fumbled in my pocket for the money, and as she was giving me the change the African girl returned to also pay her bill. I looked at her face closely. She was exceptionally beautiful. I looked at her nose, lips, forehead, and chin, everything on her face. I was going to examine the rest of her front view, but the teller said "Your groceries, sir, bye, have a good evening."

She said this while placing the bag of groceries in my hands. She must have realized my problem. Love at first sight!

As I walked through the automatic doors, I deliberately walked on her side and asked her, "Excuse me madam, are you from Africa?" She looked at me, and I suddenly feared that she was going to simply walk away and think I was looking down upon her by thinking she was African while she came from the richest country in the world, the leader of the "civilised" world – America.

She did not walk away. She smiled and said, "What makes you think I am from Africa?"

I answered sheepishly, "I am sorry, I am from Africa myself, and I thought I could pick up an African accent anywhere, even in Boston. I heard you talk to the teller, you have an African accent all right. I am your brother from Africa – Tanzania." "My name is Fred", I continued, "What is yours?"

She said her name was Betty. She did not simply say Betty like you and I would. She said "Be-tt-y", stressing the "Be" and the "tt" and immediately I knew she was from Uganda. I told her so, and she wondered how I knew. I told her that only people from Uganda pronounced Betty the way she did. We immediately got to know and like each other. We exchanged addresses and telephone numbers and promised to get together some time. I asked her if it was all right if I called her the next day, and she said she would not mind.

That evening, as I cooked and ate my supper, I was thinking of Betty. After supper, I tried to read my books but I could not concentrate, so I decided to go to bed. I could not sleep. No girl had ever made me lose my sleep, but this particular night I kept on waking up at night and thinking of Betty. I kept on seeing her. I guess this was because I had been starved of love and company since I left my home.

Saturday afternoon I telephoned her. Her sing-song voice on the telephone was so sweet. We talked for a very long time, the longest I had ever spoken on the phone. Although I had a phone installed in my flat, I had nobody to call and often nobody called me. We agreed that she would come to visit me on Monday afternoon, because I would have no classes. But even if I had classes I would have skipped them because, afterall, I had attended a lot of classes in my lifetime. Betty was more important than classes.

The next day Betty came to visit. I had spent a lot of time cleaning the apartment, preparing for Betty's visit. I even bought air freshener which I forgot to use. I must say that I had never used air freshener before because my Msasani Peninsula home always smelt nice. What with the wind from the sea, the Jacaranda trees around the house and the roses in front of the house! The windows were always open to let in the air from the sea and the sweet aroma of the flowers. Here in U.S.A. I was living in an airtight apartment.

I waited for Betty anxiously, like a boy waiting for his first date, and when she arrived I was all confused as to what to say to her. I got two glasses of chilled wine from the fridge. I was not a good host. In my Msasani home Mzee Juma would help to entertain when I had visitors, but now I had to do it myself. I was glad I was not going to make a meal for Betty, I was not much of a cook. Betty said to my relief that she already had had lunch.

Although I had spent a lot of time on cleaning the apartment, it was not clean enough. Betty must have realized that I had tried to clean it in a hurry and did not make a good job of it. She was hardly five minutes in the studio before she went to work. I protested, but she answered, "You African men are not used to house chores." So she cleaned the floor, brushed the carpet and promised to buy me a second hand vacuum cleaner to get the carpet as clean as new. She washed the dirty dishes I had forgotten in the kitchen sink after my lunch. She even inspected the dishes I had washed and rewashed them. She remade the bed, put my clothes in the right places and rearranged the books on the shelf. The place looked habitable again.

Betty did not stay long though. She had to go to her evening classes at Simon's College. As we walked side by side down Longwood Avenue and up Brooklyn Avenue to the main gate of Simon's College I felt young again. It reminded me of my adolescent days in the primary school when we used to escort girls to school.

At the gate I gave her the books I had been carrying for her and kissed her goodbye. "Thanks for the afternoon, I

82

have enjoyed being at your place. I will give you a ring from my working place," she said.

I was actually the one to thank her. She did not know that I was so lonely and lost in that lonesome city of America. If I had not met her, the loneliness and the racial atmosphere would have driven me crazy. Alternatively, I would have returned home. What would people in my office think of me? They would perhaps think that the Assistant Principal Secretary had failed his examinations.

As I walked back to my studio apartment, I felt refreshed. I felt like a dying person who had been given a new lease of life. Sitting in my studio that evening, I felt very happy with myself. I no longer felt lonely. I felt Betty's presence all the time. I had been granted a new lease of life. I had never realized how much human contact meant while in Dar es Salaam, as I was always surrounded by people. You have to feel lonely in a foreign city like I did to be able to appreciate how important human contact is!

The next day, as I arrived from school, I found the telephone ringing. It was Betty, of course. "Come over," I said. "But I cannot guarantee you some supper. We shall go to eat out because I am not so much of a cook."

Later, she arrived with some warm pizza and a bottle of Bolla wine. We ate the pizza and washed it down with the wine and watched TV while holding hands.

When she left that evening, I returned to my desk which was littered with text books, notebooks and drafts of term papers. I worked late into the night. I seemed to have acquired new vigour to work hard at my studies.

From then on, Betty became my constant companion. We would spend most of our time together. Every Sunday we would go to church together, walk in the parks or watch a movie.

We would walk in the Boston Common holding hands.

We walked the Freedom Trail and visited the site of the Boston Tea Party.

Very often she would treat me to a movie. We liked frequenting the Arlington, Brooklyn or Harvard Square theaters. I always protested when she paid for the tickets, but she would say, "Do not bother to pay, after all you are a student and I work, although in a supermarket."

It was not like in Dar es Salaam where I used to take girls to the movies at Empress on Samora Avenue and New Chox on Nkrumah Street. I would always pay even when some of the girls were earning salaries almost equal to mine. To me there was no such a thing as being treated to a movie by a lady. I always paid. But that is how society is – I mean African society. In our society the man always paid. The woman would perhaps feel that she was taking away the man's pride if she paid. She might feel that she was belittling the man and embarrassing him. In a male dominated society the man was the bread earner. He was supposed to have money and so he was supposed to foot all the bills.

When I said this to Betty she remarked that it was not fair. "After all there are female executives earning more than men," she said," Don't you get treated to dinner or a movie by a lady back home?" she asked.

I told her, "Actually I had at the Kilimanjaro Hotel. But when it came to paying she transferred the money to me under the table. She thought that even if she was paying, the money must always come from the man."

I will never forget the day we went to see the movie *"From 9 to 5"* where Dolly Parton acts as the secretary to a wife cheating boss. The boss loved the secretary and bought her things. After the movie I told Betty that the secretary reminded me of Miriam back home. She was also as beautiful as Dolly Parton, but our relationship was not the kind we saw in the film.

"Do not feel guilty, after all you are not married," Betty said.

That was Betty, always understanding, though she did not actually understand the kind of relationship that Miriam and I had.

After the movie we went to an Italian cold-sub place and ordered for "a pork-sub with everything on it" including lots of salad. Then we walked up the street eating and talking with full mouths. We did not look civilized eating in the streets, but in the free society of Boston everybody ate in the streets. I remarked to Betty that I could not dare do this type of thing while walking down Samora Avenue in Dar es Salaam. People would think I was crazy.

At Harvard square on a Sunday afternoon we watched 'The Graduate', in which a beautiful wife of a rich man, falls deeply in love with the young son of the husband's business partner.

When they were getting married, I whispered to Betty, "That will be us if all goes well."

She answered, "Look at him, proposing to me in a movie theater," and blew a kiss at me.

Chapter 7

The assasination attempt

Usually a class seated waiting for a professor to come and start a session is noisy but ours was not. On this afternoon while waiting for the professor to come in, students were involved in revising the previous day's lecture. Others were discussing in low tones the important points the professor had mentioned in the previous lecture. Other students were involved in setting up their tape recorders ready to record the lecture as soon as the professor opened his mouth to speak. Recording lectures was common in our class. Sometimes there were as many recorders in class as the number of students. A few students, like myself that afternoon, just sat quietly, not thinking of anything in particular. The professor was never late but this day he was ten minutes late. When he came in he had bad news for us.

"President Reagan has been shot at", he said in a matter-of-fact way. "He is in hospital, it has just been announced on TV."

"Is he all right?" asked one female student, with a look of alarm on her face.

"He is alive, that is all the TV announcer could tell us. Look fellows, lets get on with today's lecture, we are already late."

As if nothing had happened, he went on to expound on what makes the American chemical industry a great success in a capitalist mode of production. The lecture as usual went on with a lot of enthusiastic exchange between the students and the professor. It did not mean that because the President had been shot at lectures at Massachusetts College of Economics had to stop.

It took me four times as long to open the door that

evening. I was clumsily fumbling with the door knob, partially because I was opening it in a hurry, to get into the apartment and turn on the TV to listen to the news about the shooting, and partly because they had fixed a new lock that I had not yet known how to operate well. This type of complicated lock was fixed on all the doors in our building, after two teenagers broke into an apartment a few blocks from where I lived, woke up a nurse who was having a nap after a busy day at the Veterans' Hospital, and raped her several times. According to the police, they ran off with her money, colour TV and stereo, after stabbing her in the liver and kidney.

I turned on the TV. Bob Sternberg of ABC News was on the air, "The President is in stable condition, the rest of the victims of this heinous crime are all right except the Assistant Press Secretary to the President who is said to be unconscious. But doctors say that there are all reasons for optimism. They are doing everything to save all the lives."

I listened attentively. I was really absorbed. This was news, news about the shooting of the President of the United States. The telephone rang. I looked at the telephone in annoyance. A mysterious caller was calling my number again and when I answered, "Hello" he said "Screw yourself" and then hang up. I thought to myself, "My goodness, even the shooting of the President would not stop this fellow from making silly calls today. He must be a cousin to the person who shot the President," I thought.

I let it ring but it did not stop. Whoever was calling was determined to have me answer the phone.

I lifted it and said, "Hello!"

"I have been calling the whole evening, where were you?" It was Betty. She sounded upset. Her tone indicated that something was wrong. Of course something was wrong, the President had been shot but I did not expect Betty to take it that seriously. Even our professor and the rest of the students did not seem to be seriously affected by the shooting, and that is why the classes went on as usual.

"Fred, I am scared." I gripped the telephone preparing for the worst. Had somebody broken into her apartment and raped her? In the last four weeks there had been rape cases reported every twenty-four hours. The last had occurred in the past eight hours. A girl was abducted, forcefully thrown into a car, driven into a condominium, raped six times, beaten and dumped in the cold pavement of Massachusetts Avenue.

I could not find words to ask her what the problem was, my immediate reaction was to rush outside, call a taxi and go to her place, or maybe run fast. I felt a force that was driving me to her strong enough to let me get there faster, than a taxi could. Or maybe call the police and shout, "Rape! Murder! 995 Worthlong Street! Please hurry!"

Betty must have realised that she had scared me so she said, "Actually I am fine, only that I am a little bit shaken."

"What is wrong?" I asked.

"I am scared. They have shot the President. I am watching TV. It scares me so much. Come and stay with me."

"OK" I said, "Keep a pot of tea boiling and I will be at your door in no time."

Betty would usually not get scared easily, but tonight she was actually scared. She had stayed in U.S.A. longer than I and she knew more about the violence in the city. Murder was a household word. The media reported a lot of news on murder, shooting, larceny, stabbing, rape, arson and mugging. We had counted twenty-one discoveries of bodies of black boys under the age of ten, murdered and thrown into a river in Atlanta, Georgia. Every few days a black boy would be reported missing and a few days later he would be discovered in the river. The cause of death was strangulation. The killer, possibly a white man who hated black children, was at large and it was not known how many more black children would be killed before the killer was apprehended. When the nurse was raped and stabbed, Betty looked pretty scared when I told her the news. And she remarked, "I can see the look on her face when she woke up to find those hooligans in her flat, I can see the pain in her eyes as they raped her repeatedly and, my goodness! Imagine the look on her face as they stabbed her."

But on that day Betty did not say, "I am scared, come and stay with me."

I calmed down and quickly took a cup of coffee. I had taken to taking lots of coffee everyday. Who cared about cancer! I did not really mind drinking coffee because the evidence was not substantiated by many researchers, and after all, with all the shooting in Boston, one could go down the street and stop a bullet, so I thought, not so wisely perhaps, "but why not enjoy my coffee and die of cancer?"

A man suspected of shooting at the President had been captured. He would be arraigned before the court the following day. I turned off the TV and headed for Betty's place.

I left the house in a hurry, and as I turned the key in my new lock for the third time, I heard the telephone ringing again. Although it had started to rain outside, I walked fast down the street. I thought something was happening to Betty and that was why she was ringing again. With all these people hanging around, one is not safe even in one's own flat.

Betty received me with smiles, tea and crackers. She did not look scared as she had sounded on the phone. We discussed the shooting. How sad it was that the President had been in office for barely two months before an attempt was made on his life. Betty sounded concerned, but she was in good spirits all the same.

Her controlled mood did not last long though.

"And now let's again see the videotape of the shooting," said Bob Steinberg of the ABC News. Then we saw on TV the shooting of the President of the United States as it had occured that afternoon. The President waved to the people on his left and turned to his right with all the pomp of a president while giving them that presidential smile. All of a sudden there was a shot, and then a second shot. It looked as if the president had been hit. He bent to enter his car while still looking around to see what was happening. He did not dive cowardly into the car. It seemed as if he wanted to see his assailant, as if he wanted to identify him later if asked, "Is this the fellow who took a shot at you?"

Realizing that he was not getting into the car fast enough, security men pushed him in, sandwiched him and before the doors of the car closed, the car shot down the street heading for Washington Memorial Hospital.

The sidewalk seemed to be littered with bodies. A lot of things were happening at the same time. A machine gun totting man appeared from nowhere. He propped himself against a wall and, in half a second, he had scanned his black machine gun a hundred and eighty degrees trying to spot the gunman in the crowd to presumably shoot him before he fired any more shots.

A bulky, bald headed gentleman lay on the side walk bleeding from a head wound. He was the Assistant Press Secretary to the President. Men with first aid kits appeared from nowhere and began to administer to the injured, giving them first aid, cardiac massage and mouth to mouth resuscitation. Ambulances were on the site in less than a minute and began to take the injured away. It was an unbelievable sight. One could not believe that he was seeing the actual shooting of the President of U.S.A. It looked like a Hollywood movie.

"Now ladies and gentlemen the same picture again in slow motion," Bob came on the air again and repeated the videotape of the shooting in slow motion. I looked at Betty. She was very sad, almost crying.

When we came to the part showing the Assistant Press Secretary bleeding from the head wound, she could not hold out any more, she suddenly burst out and started to cry.

I held her in my arms, stroked her back and said, "Betty, why do you take this thing so personally. I assure you there are very few Americans crying at this time, although I am sure they love their president. They are trying to control their emotions. Violence is part of this society. I don't see why a beautiful girl from Uganda should be crying over the shooting of the President of United States, while most of the Americans are going on with their normal life as if nothing has happened."

"I am not crying for the president," Betty said, tears running down her beautiful cheeks, "I am crying for my father."

"I don't understand," I said.

Betty went on to explain to me, "The bald headed man lying on the sidewalk with the brains blown off reminds me of my father and what they did to him in Uganda."

Up to now Betty had told me very little about herself. I did not know much about her, and yet every time I looked at her, I felt that behind those smiles and beautiful eyes there was a history of emotional shock. She was very secretive. It took the shooting of the president and the presidential aide to touch the part of Betty's heart that had treasured the tragic moment of her lifetime, the moment she had tried to forget but could not.

Betty revealed to me that she was the daughter of a former Minister of Lands in Uganda. Her father, John Mukasa was a very religious man. He came from the Baganda tribe in Southern Uganda and he was very educated. He was educated at Makerere University, a highly respected institute of learning where his son also graduated with B.A. (Hons.). He did not want his daughter to go to Makerere though. He wanted her to go overseas to acquire foreign education. After all, he had only two children so if one graduated from Makerere why not have the other one study in U.K or U.S.A.?

So when Father Francis Mcmahon, his parish priest, volunteered to find a college for Betty in U.S.A. he was more than happy. Being a frequent church goer and a great supporter of the church, Betty's father was on very good terms with the priest, who sometimes thought he owed John Mukasa a favour. This is because as Minister of Lands he always helped whenever the church needed some land to build on, or when some unholy person put claim on church property.

Father Francis suggested to Betty's father that she should go to St. Francis College in Boston. "It is an excellent Catholic College. They have very good teachers and it will not cost you a thing. All her tuition was to be paid by the Catholic Diocese of Boston. All you have to do is buy her an air ticket to Boston and your daughter has three years of college education free, after which she can do a Master's Degree and even a Doctorate if she wants to."

So Betty ended up in Boston to study for a Bachelor's Degree at St. Francis College.

"I'll never forget the day I left home. I was so excited and I did not shed a tear. The only time I cried a bit was when I said goodbye to my classmates from Gayaza High School. Most of my friends were going to Makerere to do various degree courses and I was going to America. This was my first trip to U.S.A. I had been to Europe with my dad and mum, but not to U.S.A. As I hugged my parents at Entebbe Airport, I did not know that I was seeing them for the last time." Betty sadly continued to narrate.

"I am sorry Betty, why don't we leave this for another day?" I said, fearing that I was also going to shed tears. Betty was no longer crying. She was in full control of the situation and so she said, "I do not think I would like to live through it again so let me finish." She continued her story with misty

92

eyes and an occasional sob. Occasionally I would wipe a tear from her eyes, but all the same she went on. She wanted to tell it all to show how cruel some people are.

"A suspect in the shooting of the president has been captured and identified as Mike Mcnley, the son of a millionaire in Dallas," the ABC announcer said.

"Anyway, what do you expect of Dallas, isn't it where they shot and killed President Kennedy in 1963?" Betty remarked.

"So I came to study at St. Francis college." Betty continued.

"That is a very good college," I complemented.

"Thanks darling, but I was not given the opportunity to study in the college for long. You are aware, I am sure of what happened in Uganda in 1971. Well, the day Idi Amin came to power, my parents were among the first people to be killed. You know he killed many of Obote's ministers and their families. My brother, thank God, was not in the country. He was the Permanent Secretary in the Ministry of Defence and he had travelled with Dr. Obote to Singapore for the Commonwealth Conference. He is now safe in Kenya. He writes to me often to tell me that one day we will return to Uganda to avenge our parents' tragic death, but I doubt if we will.

"I got very little news about the coup. This country! There is so little foreign news. It is not even announced with sufficient details when there is a coup in an important country like Uganda was at that time. It was simply, "There has been a military coup in Uganda and a military government has taken over. The new President is Idi Amin, a Major General in the Uganda army. All the American citizens in the country are safe."

I got more news later on that night that my father and mother had been taken from our house on Mengo Hill and sent to Amin's headquarters. They were questioned, tortured and shot through the head and thrown into River Nile."

When I saw the president's aide fall onto the sidewalk, his smart suit, his bald head and his rather bulky form reminded me of my father. The head of the presidential aide looks so much like my father's. I always remember the way I used to caress the bald spot at the centre of his head. I can imagine him seated in our black Mercedes Benz, the bald spot on his head shining in the Kampala sun. God, why did you create people like Idi Amin or people like this guy - what is his name again, the crazy man who wanted to kill the president? He ended up blowing up the head of the person with a bald head like my father's."

"Something Henkley, I did not hear the name well. Anyway, like Oswald, who killed President Kennedy, we shall continue to see him in the press, in books, on TV - everywhere starting tonight, we will get sick of it," I said.

"I got sick of Idi Amin too," Betty continued. "The way the Western press loved him. Everytime he farted through his mouth it appeared on the front pages of the most popular Western papers. He killed my parents, blew their skulls with the same guns the Israelis had sold to President Obote's Government. My father had travelled with Idi Amin when Idi Amin was in command of the Armed Forces during Obote's rule to shop for the weapons he later used to kill him. He did not even give him a decent burial. He instead threw him in the Nile for crocodiles to eat. My goodness, my dad was killed and fed to crocodiles!" She broke down again and cried like a child.

I did not hear the announcer clearly saying, "According to news from Washington Memorial Hospital, the president is going to be operated on," as I turned the TV off. I had an important task to do. I had to comfort Betty, try and make her forget the sad story and stop crying.

I touched my eyes. I was also crying and I guessed that was why Betty stopped because she realized she had made me sad. She was that type of person. She did not like to make people sad.

She went to the fridge and opened some cans of Heinken beer and said, *"Tunywe mwenge"*. It was the first time since I met her that I heard her speak in Luganda. She was in control of the situation again. As she opened her mouth to speak, I put my hands on her cold lips to stop her from talking any further, and with the other hand I turned on the TV. "The president is going to undergo surgery."

"Let's hear about the operation," said Betty. "But why don't they tell us about the person who looks like my father?"

I beseeched Betty to stop talking about her father, "For sure he is in heaven, he was a good man, God loved him." I assured her.

Betty was no longer crying. She said, seriously, "If he was buried, I would have risked going home two years ago to see his grave. But perhaps Amin's soldiers would have picked me up from the airport and sent me straight to Amin's residence to be raped, killed and thrown into the Nile, like he did with my parents."

My skin developed goose bumps on hearing this. I hoped she would stop this kind of talk, but she did not.

"When I die, my tombstone will bear three names: My father's, my mother's and mine.

HERE LIE THREE OF US:

JOHN MUKASA DIED 1971

JANE MUKASA DIED 1971

BETTY NAMUKASA DIED. . .

"Well, I do not know when I will die. I hope soon. What is the use of living after what happened to my parents?"

"Betty, I love you. Do not talk about death. If you die then what is the use of me living?"

I had never told her that I loved her, though in her heart

I knew and she knew that I loved her more than I had ever loved before.

She smiled and said, "I mean it darling. I must have a grave in our parish cemetery, the burial ground which my father as the Minister for Lands demarcated for the departed faithfuls in our parish, yet he was denied a decent burial. That is where I will be buried and my tombstone will bear three names, a family of three, three in one just like the Holy Trinity – Father, Son and the Holy Ghost."

Betty was getting rather interesting, and as long as she was not crying I thought, "Why not continue with the conversation?" So I asked her, "What happened to the scholarship at St. Francis, darling?"

"Well, out of sight out of mind. In the second year after my father died, I was told that there was no more fees for me and that if I had the fees I was welcome to continue schooling. But imagine a girl, a black girl, an African girl paying her school fees and living expenses in this country. So at the end of the second year, I left college. I had registered as a refugee with the Federal Government, and so I got myself a job at the food store where I now work. What I earn plus the refugee allowance I receive from the government is enough for my rent, food and fees for evening classes at Simon's College. I hope one day I will go back to St. Francis College and finish my Degree course. I had accumulated twenty five credits. I need fifteen more to get my Bachelor's Degree, but what shall I do with it? In this country there are many unemployed people, or people working at gas stations, yet they have university degrees. The best I can do with mine is to work in a store which is what I am doing now anyway, the daughter of a Government Minister."

I feared she might start the story anew, so, again, I turned on the TV. "The president is still in the theatre. We have no news yet of what happened to the Press Secretary," said the announcer.

"I think he is dead," Betty said, sadly. "My father did not live, not with half of his skull blown off, but that was in Uganda. I am told that Idi Amin used to eat the kidneys and liver of his victims, and one cannot live without these organs, let alone the brain."

I thought it best to get Betty out of the house and so I suggested that we go to Arby's for hamburger and coke and talk about something else.

At Arby's nobody was talking about the shooting. People were quietly eating their hamburgers as usual. We had our hamburgers and french fries too. When we returned, the president had already come out of theatre and to Betty's relief, it was announced that the man who looked like her father had had head surgery and was recovering from anaesthesia.

Chapter 8

Winter and Death

The weather grew colder and colder everyday, and soon the beauty of autumn was replaced by the ugliness of winter. Then came the first snowfall of the season. One day we had to leave school early after the professor declared with enthusiasm before the last lecture ended, "Look fellows, there is news of the first snowstorm, the earliest we have ever had in Boston during this season since 1930, so let us close shop early."

Back in my lonely studio, I put some supper on the stove. I looked out of the window. The glass window was misty from the boiling supper. It was cold to the touch, everywhere, it was as cold as ever. Outside, the first snow flakes were already falling silently and gently. There was something weird about the way the snow flakes were falling – the slowness, the gentleness, the quietness. I stood at the window for a long time watching this ghostly scene!

Soon there was a fine thin layer of the white stuff everywhere on the sidewalks, in the street, on top of the parked cars, on the garbage heap across the street. There was snow everywhere.

At this time the street was deserted, except for a young lady bundled in a heavy woollen winter coat, mittens and a hood. She was plodding carefully down the street. I watched her as she came down the street, a lonely figure walking in the 5 p.m. semi-darkness of Boston. From the hood to the heels of her high heeled shoes she was sprinkled with snow flakes. The shoes were giving her a hell of a problem in walking through the layer of snow that had just formed on the sidewalk. She must have got a feeling that someone was watching her. As she passed my window she quickly shifted her gaze from the road to my window. In the process she tripped and almost fell. I saw her lips form the word, "shit". The curse was almost loud enough for me to hear. She quickly steadied herself and continued to walk down the street, leaving small shoe marks in the snow.

Winter nights are long, lonely and cold. One becomes weary of spending nights alone. After my supper, consisting of boiled potatoes, a piece of pork and hot soup, I retired early in my cold tiny studio apartment to try and forget about my loneliness.

However, it is difficult for a student to have an undisturbed, peaceful, all-night-sleep, with unread readings and unfinished homework hanging over him, so I got up at 3 a.m, sat at my table and started working.

At 5 a.m. I drew my curtains open. Outside it was all snow. Everything was covered with snow. People were already out with shovels clearing snow from driveways.

Schools were closed since buses could not take children to school because of the slippery roads. Such a thing had happened to us too in 1950, when we were in middle school. We also missed school, not because of snow but because the river that runs between our village and the school was flooded due to the heavy December rains.

This winter was exceptionally cold, the coldest winter they had had in Boston for 30 years. Temperatures stayed below freezing point most of the time.

During winter many people die. They die mostly of pneumonia. It happens more often to those living alone in apartments that are not well heated. It often happens to old people because they suffer often from flu and other respiratory ailments more frequently than younger people. Everybody, somehow, gets sick during winter, and that is why many people keep swallowing vitamin pills believing that they make the body strong and prevent one from getting sick.

This was not Betty's first winter in U.S.A., but all the same she developed pneumonia. In January, during a particularly cold week, she began to cough and complain of chest pains. At first it was only an occasional cough, a dry cough, and we thought it would disappear. Later as the cough came on more often and she complained of chest pains, I thought it was something serious and that she should see a doctor.

Betty thought it was only flu and that she would get over it. "It is that store I work in. It is not well heated and I keep on getting flu every winter," she complained.

So, the next day we left her apartment for Holyoke Centre at Harvard Square where her doctor had an office. We got on the Train at Simphony station. The underground was congested that Friday afternoon. Everybody was wrapped up in warm clothes. Just as we entered the underground we saw a white schoolboy singing and playing his guitar. A tin, now half full with quarters from admirers, was placed in front of him and more people were throwing money into it. A few yards from him another singer, a black blind man was also singing and playing sweet tunes from a mouth organ. There were only five nickels in his tin.

A whiteman remarked, "Why doesn't he go down south to sing his slave songs?"

On the train Betty looked tired and feverish. A white man gave her his seat to the amazement of his white girlfriend, who eyed him with contempt and moved out of her seat to my advantage. I took the seat and sat beside Betty and let her head rest on my shoulder.

At Holyoke Centre we sat in the doctor's waiting room. Patients were reading newspapers and various pamphlets that doctors put in their waiting rooms to help patients relax. While Betty sat reading the *Boston Globe*, I read one of the medical journals. I found an article about death due to heart attack during love making. The article said that of the

100

married men who had heart attack while making love, three quarters got the attack while making love with partners other than their wives. I thought this was a silly article. But the next one surprised me more. It said that efforts were being made to prove that black people were less intelligent than white people. It had to do with the gene for intelligence. Some white scientist claimed to have found the gene for intelligence absent in many more black people than white people. I threw the paper down in disgust.

Betty was not in the mood for conversation. She seemed to be thinking of something. Having nothing to do I tried to listen to the little conversation that was going on in various corners of the waiting room. A teenage girl was explaining to her friend that she was going to the doctor to have her I.U.D. removed for it was giving her excessive bleeding.

"I think I will have to go on the pill this time," she concluded.

I stopped listening and watched the nurse who appeared at the door from time to time to welcome patients into the doctor's room. She would escort the patient to the door and stay there to smile at the next patient if he or she was white or just stand there till the next patient entered if he or she was black. It really did not matter to me if she smiled or cried when Betty entered. All that mattered to me was that my Betty be declared fit, or sick with something minor.

I sat worrying in the outer office when Betty entered the doctor's room. After some time she emerged from the doctor's office looking weak and sick.

The doctor escorted her out and came to talk to me, "She has pneumonia in the lower lobe of the right lung. I am hopeful it will clear up with penicillin. The pneumococcus, the causative organism of pneumonia is very sensitive to penicillin. We shall admit her into Massachusetts General Hospital and give her some shots. She will be OK after a few days," he assured me.

We took a taxi to Massachusetts General Hospital. In the

taxi, Betty looked sick. Nevertheless she was smiling.

I must also have looked very unhappy and that is why Betty said to me, "Do not worry, as the doctor said I shall recover soon."

She handed me the keys to her flat and asked me to finish washing the dishes she had left in the sink.

"Do not eat all the food in the house," she joked.

At Massachusetts General Hospital we were received by an elderly nurse. She was all smiles. She had been telephoned that we were on our way there. She immediately took us to a room that Betty was to share with another lady. The nurse put Betty to bed, explained to her how to operate the lights, the telephone, the TV and how to put her bed in the reclining position. She added, "Anyway you will not have to change the position of your bed. Because you have pneumonia we shall have to prop you up in bed for your own comfort."

Then a young doctor appeared.

"My name is Dr. Greyson, I am in charge of the medical admission on this floor. Please sit up in bed and answer a few questions," he said to Betty.

I asked him if I should go out into the lobby.

"No," he said. "Stay on. I understand you are a close friend of hers, you might be useful as I talk to her. You can leave when I begin to examine her."

He was very polite. He went on to ask Betty things like, when did the cough start? How much sputum did she cough? Did she have chest pain? Had she ever had TB? Betty answered the questions without difficulty but as she was explaining about the pain, she got an attack. She coughed and coughed while I held her. Three nurses came to her side, told me not to worry and held her instead, while I sadly sat in front of her. She put both her hands on my laps and continued to cough while the nurses supported her and patted her back.

She coughed till her whole body was covered in sweat. A

nurse rushed to bring a mug for Betty to spit into and another one wiped her face with a cold towel.

"Take it easy dear," Dr. Greyson said, "May I examine you now?"

I went out into the visitor's room and sat sadly in a chair. One of the nurses came to talk to me. I must have looked very unhappy and she thought I needed a few words of comfort.

When Dr. Greyson finished, he came to talk to me. He was also very hopeful and told me the same things the doctor at Holyoke Centre had said. But that is the way doctors behave. Always hopeful. And even when they see a hopeless condition they do not say it, because their hearts are soft. Moreover, some diseases confuse doctors such that they can tell you that you will be on your feet again, soon, only for you to die the next day.

Visiting time was over. I had to leave Betty. They had already started her on penicillin. She had taken some soup and was lying propped up in bed. I asked her whether or not I should telephone her brother in Nairobi and tell him that she was in hospital but she told me not to. She did not want to worry him.

"After all, I am going to be out of here in no time. The doctor said I only have a touch of pneumonia."

That was Betty. She did not want to make others unhappy and she did not want to bother her brother in Nairobi, even when she was lying in hospital.

I kissed her 'goodbye' and left. She managed a smile as I walked to the door and when I reached the door she blew me a kiss.

Next morning before I went to school, I telephoned the hospital. Betty told me that she had slept very well.

"In fact the nurses came to wake me up to give me a sleeping pill that I did not need," she said. But she went on to tell me that the pain in the chest was getting worse and that she had once woken up coughing terribly but that I ought not to worry.

"I'll be OK," she said and repeated that she loved me.

"Go to school and work at your studies. Remember you must pass your exams and go back home, to become a Principal Secretary."

After school I went to the hospital again. When I arrived on the floor where Betty was admitted, the same nurse who had welcomed us the previous day rushed to me.

"Oh! Fred, I am so glad to see you. Betty was asking to see you. I telephoned but you were not at home. I guessed you must have been on your way, coming this way."

"How is she?" I asked. I could barely hear myself.

"She is a little bit worse, go and see her. I'll get the doctor to talk to you," she said, ushering me into Betty's room.

Betty was propped up in bed. She looked sick and breathless. I could not imagine that she was the same Betty I had come with to the hospital the previous day. She did have a touch of pneumonia then, but apparently, she now had a fulminating type of pneumonia.

She was now attached to all sorts of monitors. A monitor for blood pressure, heart function, pulse, temperature and respiration. She had a drip in her right hand and she was on oxygen. Wires and tubes criss-crossed her bed in all directions. Machines monitored her progress and all the data was being fed into computers. That is modern medicine or computerized medical care. Two nurses were attending to her. I sat beside her. One of them took the oxygen mask from her nose and said, "She can talk to you but if she becomes worse please put on the oxygen mask like this and press the red button here."

Betty looked at me with half open eyes. She was breathless and tired. It was difficult to believe that she could have gone downhill that fast. It was only yesterday that she walked into the hospital and now she was moribund! I touched her forehead. She took my hand in her free hand and pressed it. She wanted to demonstrate that she was still strong and that I should also be strong.

Soon Dr. Greyson appeared. "Fred I am sorry but we are doing all that we can."

He took me to his office and explained to me that Betty had what he called fulminating pneumonia caused by a virulent type of bacteria.

"This type of bacteria spreads very fast in the lungs. Yesterday only one lobe of the lung was affected. This morning all the lobes, except the left upper lobe, are affected." He went on to show me the X-rays, though I had never looked at any X-ray in my life.

"You see looking at chest X-rays can be very easy. Here, the white areas are what we call opacities. They are all abnormal except, of course, in the centre where you see the whiteness representing the location of the heart. You see most of the lungs, except that black area in the left upper side, look white while they should look dark. This shows that she has fulminating pneumonia affecting the whole right lung and most of the left lung."

It seemed that Dr. Greyson was preparing me for the worst.

"What are the chances Doctor?" I asked, really worried. "In Medicine, we call it prognosis." He seemed to be giving me a lecture in medicine instead of talking about Betty's condition.

"We cannot tell the prognosis now. We have started her on the best antibiotics and we are running tests to determine the sensitivity of the organism. Rest assured that we are doing our best. At Massachusetts General Hospital we have the best chest physicians in the State and perhaps in the whole of United States."

I returned to Betty's bed and sat, holding her hand. We remained quiet for a long time, looking into each others eyes, each of us wondering what was going on inside the others mind.

Betty looked pale, her lips were dry. She rolled her dry tongue on her dry lips and attempted to speak.

"Please Betty just lie still. You are not strong enough to talk. Just speak to me through your beautiful eyes and I can hear you very well," I said incoherently. I could not look at her eyes when she started to speak. I listened to her without knowing that these were to be her last words.

"Take my body home, love. Father McMahon is still at Mpigi Mission, he will see that I am buried in my family's burial ground in my father's coffee and banana plantations. Tell my uncle that I love him and may God bless him. I love you, Fred, and I would have loved to be your wife, to bear and raise your children, but God, who knows best, has decided to take me away from you. You will find another wife, God willing."

Her voice was getting faint, I could barely hear her. While she was talking I held my head in my hands. I could not believe that I was hearing those words from Betty's lips. It could have been somebody else, but not Betty.

I looked at her. As our eyes met she smiled. I wanted to cry. Then her lips parted again and she said, "Fred remember you are a man, an African man, and African men have strong hearts. Be strong. I love you and do not disappoint me by being weak when I really need you to be strong."

She closed her lips and eyes. She could not talk any more. I murmured something that I cannot remember very well but I think it was, "Betty you are not going to die. You are going to recover and be strong again. We shall get married right here in Boston and go back to Tanzania, where we shall live happily till death do us part."

I kissed her lips. They were cold and dry.

Soon the bell rang, visiting time was over. Seeing the grief and pain on my face, the nurse escorted me to the door.

At the door she held my hand in both of hers. Her hands

were very warm. I wished they were Betty's hands. She said to me, "Do not worry too much, she might recover." With that she closed the gate of Massachusetts General Hospital behind me and I walked into the cold evening, already engulfed by loneliness and pain.

I cannot remember how I got home. All I remember now is that the telephone was ringing as I opened the door into my studio.

"Is that Fred?" The nurses's voice said.

I answered, "Yes this is Fred."

"This is Massachusetts General Hospital. I am sorry I have bad news for you. Betty has passed away," she broke the news.

I held the receiver for long, unable to speak, while she kept on saying, "Fred are you there?" till she finally gave up and replaced the phone.

As I write, I can still see Betty's face as it was that January evening, the last time I saw her alive. I can still hear her last words. Even in her death bed where I should have been the one to give her comfort and encouragement, she was the one who was encouraging me to be bold and strong. I can still see and feel those dry cold lips. It is impossible to believe that she is dead and gone forever, into eternity.

I sat on my bed and cried. I cannot remember for how long, but I cried until I could cry no more. I was grieved and all alone. There was nobody to comfort me and tell me to take it easy or even cheat me with such words like, "It is all right just take it easy," even though it was not possible. How could I take it easy when I had lost my companion, my lover and my future wife.

I was too confused to deal with the grief and the emptiness of being separated from Betty. I could not think, see or hear.

How I got to Betty's apartment I cannot remember. I found myself in her apartment sitting on her bed trying to think with my head held in between my hands. Betty's apartment was the ideal place to sit and think of what to do.

Betty's one bedroom apartment looked empty and large without her. The apartment seemed to have all of a sudden, grown a hundred times its size. The bed was neatly made as she had left it, but her books and notebooks lay carelessly on the table. An unfinished letter lay on her desk. She was writing to her brother. Her address and telephone notebook lay on the table. I opened it and found her brother's telephone number in Nairobi. It was now 10 p.m. and 5 a.m. in Kenya, so I thought I would not get him out of bed with the terrible news about the death of his sister. I decided to call in an hour's time. It would then be 6 a.m. East African Standard Time.

Betty's telephone rang. By then I had found her insurance papers. It was the hospital. They had tried to contact me and failing to do so they decided to try Betty's place. They wanted to know what to do with the body.

The insurance papers had a clause, "In the occurrence of death, we will pay for the cost of getting rid of the remains at a cost not exceeding three thousand dollars." It was something terrible and funny to put in an insurance contract but there it was. I thought the insurance people use terrible language but the language was not my concern. I was glad there was enough money perhaps to send Betty's body home for burial. I told them that I would call a funeral home to claim the body.

In U.S.A. funeral service costs are very high. It is not like back home in Tanzania, where, when somebody dies, friends, relatives and even people who did not know the deceased would contribute money for the funeral arrangements. Here you must arrange for your funeral before you die, and that is where insurance companies and funeral homes come in handy.

During our walks with Betty in Boylston, we had passed

108

by a very beautiful funeral home. In fact Betty had remarked when we passed by it, "What a beautiful place!"

"It is a funeral home," I said.

"A funeral home or not, it is beautiful all the same!" She had concluded.

So I called Quiet Slumber Funeral Home and asked them to pick up the body. I told them that I would contact them in the morning.

At 6.20 a.m. East African Standard Time, I rang Ben Mukasa in Nairobi. He was still in bed. I had wondered how I was going to break the news, perhaps I would just tell it the way the hospital did – "I am sorry, Betty has passed away," I thought.

"Hello! is that Nairobi 29856?"

The voice at the other end in Africa answered, "What do you want?" I understood that Ugandans living in Kenya always shied away from talking to strangers on the phone for fear that their whereabouts would be known. "Can I talk to Ben Mukasa, please?" I said trying to suppress a sob.

The person at the other end said, "He does not live here. What is your name?"

I quickly gave him the bad news. "Listen Ben, my name is Fred. I am from Tanzania and I am talking from Boston. It is about Betty your sister." I could not suppress the sobs anymore.

"She is. . . sick, very ill," I managed to say. I could not manage to say that she was dead. I could not talk anymore. I hang up and lay on the bed.

Later he rang Betty's number, and as I answered, I knew he was prepared for the worst. So I told him the whole story about how Betty had developed pneumonia, and how her condition had quickly gone downhill and the sudden death.

"Was she murdered?" He thought Amin's killing squad had killed her.

I assured him that it was a natural death. I explained to

him that I was a civil servant from Tanzania and, that I held a responsible position back home and, that I would do my best to help. I informed him that before she died, Betty had requested that I take her body home for burial. I told him that we needed time to think of what to do. And that we ought to get in touch again later. He warned me not to telephone anybody else about the death, not even Betty's friends until we spoke again, lest the "wrong" people know of her death.

Ben and I rang each other many more times. He was a strong man. He never broke down when we talked, although sometimes I almost did, myself. He knew that this was a tough world. He had lost his parents and now his sister, he therefore must go on living, perhaps to see the day when Idi Amin would die.

We agreed that I should take the body home. He had already contacted his uncle and relatives in Uganda and a cousin of his was sneaking back into Uganda to prepare for the funeral. We agreed that I would telephone to tell him when I would be met at the airport by only two or three people in order to avoid publicity.

I was glad school had closed for ten days on mid-term holiday. I could travel to Uganda, lay Betty to rest and return, though late to continue with my studies. I had read to Ben the names of Betty's friends from her address and telephone book and he told me who to contact and who not to contact. Her friends came to see me. We assembled at Betty's place everyday, consoling each other. I was no longer lonely, although I was very grieved. However, when everybody left, I would stay awake the whole night thinking of Betty, not believing that she was dead and gone for ever.

Chapter 9

From America to Africa with Betty's Body

I was booked on flight number LH 350 to London. There was no direct flight to Entebbe. "We do not fly to Entebbe directly as we used to during the days before Idi Amin. We always fly to Nairobi first to investigate if things are OK in Uganda. While there, we first get information on any serious developments in Uganda like a coup attempt, war, shooting, looting or hostage-taking at the airport. We have to find out all these things before we fly into Entebbe." The lady at the booking desk had explained to me at length.

"Uganda is unpredictable," I added.

After I had booked the sweet voice with a German accent signed off with, " Have a nice day."

"You, too," I answered, because I was sure that she would definitely have a nice day even if I did not wish her one. But on my part I definitely would have a sad day even if she wished me a nice day a hundred times. With Betty dead, I was sure I would never have a nice day in this life. There would be no more sunshine in my life.

I called the mortician to ask him to book Betty's body on flight LH 350 and inform the booking office that I was escorting the body. The mortician accepted, and said he would bring the necessary documents to my flat. I told him he need not bring the documents. I would go and pick them up from the mortuary. I wanted to see Betty's body again, I wanted to be near her.

The mortician also signed off with, "Have a nice day," and I thought that just like the Air Lufthansa booking clerk, he was wasting his time wishing me a good day.

At 5 p.m., I called a Boston cab. On an ordinary day, on an ordinary trip, I would go to the airport on the subway. I would get on the train at Simphony station to Government Centre, where I would change to the Blue Line and ride down to the station going by the name, "Airport." Here I would get on an airport bus. It is a beautiful trip especially when you come to the Blue Line where they have blue, beautiful coaches which service white South Boston. But on this particular journey to the airport I could not travel on the train. I could not stand the site of all those people kissing, hugging and caressing each other on the train as if they had no homes where they could do these things, in private. At this time, when I was sad and missing my lover, the sight of a couple holding hands, let alone kissing, would bring back memories of the good times I had had with Betty.

The journey to the airport went without a word. I did not seem to notice the 5 p.m. heavy traffic because I was in deep thought, thinking about Betty, about her body and about the coffin. Where was it now? Possibly the mortician had had it picked up already and now, as I was seated comfortably in the back seat of a Boston cab, Betty was lying at the airport luggage office, her body wrapped in white sheets in a coffin. I hoped the roses I had placed on the coffin were still there. I would like to deliver the body with the roses.

"Are you okay, sir?" The cab driver must have been watching me in the over-head mirror. He must have noticed the pain on my face. I was in terrible agony. "I am fine, thanks," I managed to say.

"Which airline, sir?" I wished he would cut off the "sir" bit.

"Lufthansa," I answered.

"Okay, Sir," that "sir" again and again. Today I seemed to mind the "sir" so much. I was sad. Even a million "sirs" would not have raised my spirits.

We made it to the airport in one hour.

The booking clerk took my ticket and smiled.

"Are you booked, sir?" Her "sir" sounded nicer than the cabbie's.

"Yes," I said.

She ran a painted finger nail down the list of passengers. I began imagining what would happen if I was not on the list and they were over-booked, so that Betty's body would have to go without me. I thought of what I would have to do. Tell them that I was accompanying a body and, that the body was already on the plane so they would have to get it off the plane, call the mortician to collect it and keep it till the next flight. The thought of staying another day in Boston, sleeping in my warm bed in my warm studio, while Betty lay in a coffin in that funeral home did not please me!

The ticket clerk took the ticket to another desk, punched information into a computer and came back smiling. "How do you spell your second name, sir?"

"M-u-n-y-a-o," I spelt.

"Can you spell that again, I am sorry," she said. I thought she did not know what being sorry means. I was the one who was sorry, sore, unhappy, and in anguish.

I spelt again for her: "M as in Mississippi, U as in unhappy, N as in New Jersey, Y as in New York, A as in America, O as in New Orleans." She smiled back at me. The smile was so tantalizing, so sweet and so wide that it even showed a gold filing in her last molar. It was an infectious smile. I could not help but smile too. My first smile since Betty's death.

"Do you have any luggage?" she asked.

I almost blurted, "It has been checked in already." The thought of referring to Betty as luggage nauseated me.

"I only have this handbag," I declared.

"Welcome aboard," the tall smiling cabin attendant told me. I wished they had said that to Betty, too, when they had taken her to the luggage cabin – but, poor Betty, they had probably just wheeled her in like any other luggage.

Soon I found myself seated between two gentlemen, a Dane and the other I could not quite place. He could have been a German because he spoke very beautiful German with the air hostess. And then I began to wonder how I could sit there in the reclining seat with earphones listening to music and being served with food and drinks by a beautiful air hostess, while Betty lay in the luggage cabin?

I wished she was seated by me. I closed my eyes and imagined her seated on my left side. The Danish gentleman with a grey beard was Betty! I imagined her alive with her long elegant neck, her smile, snow white teeth and lipsticked lips, conversing intelligently and gently and as usual pronouncing her B's and T's with a Baganda accent. The accent from the country she had left seven years ago, expecting to go back to her God loving parents. I imagined her in my arms hugging and kissing her. She would always insist that we stop before we spoilt the joy reserved for our wedding night. I could not go on imagining for fear that I might in my sleep, without knowing it, hug and kiss the person seated on my left side thinking it was Betty. He would surely complain to the cabin attendant and have his seat changed, because he would have thought that he was seating with a very funny person – probably a homosexual.

I opened my eyes and looked into the eyes of the air hostess.

"Shall I fasten your seat belt for you, sir? You look tired and sleepy."

"No, madam, I will do it myself, thanks," I said.
She straightened my seat and smiled. I wished life were only smiles.

The air hostess went into the formalities of, "The oxygen bag is in the bag in front of your seat, the oxygen terminals are. . ."

She demonstrated how to use the oxygen mask. I was not

114

paying much attention until she demonstrated how to use the life jacket.

"In case of an emergency we shall ask you to wear the life jacket. Open it thus and wear it over your front."

I was watching but not quite hearing her. I was thinking of what would happen if we crushed. We would wear the life jackets and hopefully land in the Atlantic Ocean, where we would perhaps float waiting for help. Nobody would mind about the luggage, including Betty's coffin. The coffin would perhaps open and Betty would be eaten by sharks or if the airplane caught fire she would burn into ashes. Perhaps that would be a better way of burying her, her ashes spread all over the Atlantic ocean. But that is not the way she wanted to be buried. She wanted to be laid to rest in her homeland, in her parish.

While all these thoughts were running through my mind I knew the other passengers were also not paying attention to what the air hostess was saying about the safety precautions. While I was preoccupied with Betty's body, the male passengers were admiring the sensuous lips of the air hostess and her well formed breasts which bulged through the jacket. She finished and walked down the alley to see that all passengers were ready for the take off. Then the voice of the pilot came on the air, first in German then in English to introduce himself and to tell us how glad he was to fly us to London. He then wished us a pleasant flight and told us that if there was anything we needed, we could call the attendants who would be too glad to help.

"Have a pleasant trip. Just relax and enjoy yourself," he signed off.

But there was one person who was not enjoying herself; Betty in the luggage cabin.

Dinner, consisting of veal, french fries, baked beans, salad and apple pie was served. I could not eat, I just looked at it. The smell of food did not appeal to me since Betty's death. The gentlemen seated on either side of me ate their dinner and drank a lot of wine and German beer, while I only drank a coke. When the air hostess came to take away my untouched dinner her eyes seemed to be saying, "Why didn't you tell me that you were not going to eat?"

The German gentleman tried to engage me in conversation. "Where are you from?" he asked.

"Tanzania. Do you know where that is?" I asked him.

"I have not been there but of course I have heard a lot about it. Isn't that the country where you have a great president, Mwalimu Julius Nyerere, one of the greatest presidents in Africa? I read a lot about your president."

He continued to tell me that he had a brother who worked in a hospital in Zimbabwe during the liberation war.

"I like the way Mugabe is running Zimbabwe, trying his best to be in the middle. They have unfairly branded him a Marxist."

I wanted to say that there was nothing wrong with being a Marxist but I was in no mood for a discussion on Marxism. He continued to talk about the Cuban troops in Angola, and how much he liked the president of Mozambique.

When travelling by air you often travel with people who do not like to talk. They sit there drowned as I was today in their own thoughts and troubles or in their own work and pleasures. I once sat on a plane for eight hours by the side of a person who could not say a word except, "Oh!" when I accidentally stepped on his toe while passing to go to the toilet. I like people who talk, but today I was in no mood for conversation.

How is it that when you need and would very much enjoy something it just does not come your way, but when you do not want it and when it would be a bother, it comes along? Like that dull flight when I was going to U.S.A. I sat near a guy who all the way sat upright in his chair and did not say a word the whole trip. He just sat there eating, drinking and reading a novel with a naked girl on the cover. What was a sixty year old man doing with a novel like that? I had wanted to talk most on that trip because I wanted to hear more about U.S.A. The only information I had about U.S.A. was from Chief and he could have seen only one side of it. Moreover it was difficult to change all of a sudden from the conversational world of Dar es Salaam to a world where people were mute. I really needed somebody to talk to then.

That night, on my way to London, when I least wanted somebody to talk to, here was a guy talking to me about his worries, regarding Cuban troops in Angola, Zimbabwe being neutral and governing well and about his great doctor brother who worked in Zimbabwe.

I listened to songs by Cliff Richard and the late Elvis Presley - *"You look like an angel ..."* After some time I slept, but not for long, because soon we were woken up and given hot towels to freshen up with. It was now barely mid-night by American time but on the other side of the Atlantic, where we were now approaching, it was almost day break.

The gentleman on my right complained, "Why not let us sleep for goodness sake?"

I was more disturbed about being woken up into a world where there was no Betty. I wished the air hostess had let me sleep on. I wished I could sleep forever. What was the use of waking up when Betty had slept into eternity?

Breakfast was served and although it was barely four hours after we had had our dinner, my colleagues' appetites unlike mine were very good. Breakfast was splendid as usual – cottage cheese, salad, Italian bread, a large orange, grapes, scrambled eggs and a lot of hot tea. To occupy myself, I drank all the tea and unwrapped all the utensils and food from the cellophane covering and replaced them on the tray. I could not eat. It was not like my flight to U.S.A. months ago, when I had eaten everything they offered me on the plane and arrived having gained a kilo in less than twenty four hours.

It was 5.30 a.m. Outside, the sun was rising from the sea. It was a beautiful sunrise. I wished Betty were there to see the beauty of the sunrise but she would never see any sunrise again. I wondered how many more sunrises I would live to see in my lifetime and why God had decided that I should see more sunrises while Betty would see no more. Why didn't He decide that I should not see any more and let Betty see hundreds of more sunshines?

I ended up by saying, "Thou shall not question the ways of the Lord."

That reading from my early primary school catechism classes seemed to pop up too often in my thoughts lately. I feared I was becoming a born again christian.

My thoughts were interrupted by: "Ladies and Gentlemen, good morning, this is your captain. We shall be landing at London's Heathrow Airport in fifteen minutes. The weather in London is lovely, not too hot, not too cold, just fine. So relax and continue enjoying the last minutes of your flight."

Chapter 10

Heathrow Airport

The change is obvious. There is a sharp contrast between developed and developing countries, first world and third world, in terms of resourcefulness as you travel from U.S.A. to Africa. If you travel from Washington, New York or Boston via London to Entebbe, Nairobi, Dar es Salaam etcetera in less than twenty four hours, you feel that the clock has been pushed back a century.

In fact if you are observant you do not have to travel all the way to Entebbe to feel the difference. You start to feel it at Heathrow Airport in London, as soon as you arrive at Terminus 3; the terminus for flights taking off to Arab and African countries. The signboards here read: "Somali Airlines, Ethiopia Airlines, Egyptian Airlines, Kenya Airways, Nigeria Airlines, and they are all crowded in a space just large enough be occupied by one Japanese or Pan American Plane located upstairs above terminus 3.

The ticket and luggage offices are extremely congested. Booking clerks are stationed barely a foot from each other. The little space is so much occupied with passengers and luggage that you will not have space to put your foot.

Luggage here is in plenty. You see all kinds of exotically decorated luggage from the third world, unlike the plain mono-coloured luggage you see at the other terminals. It looks like a free exhibition of African and Oriental art, but if you are not artistically oriented all that your narrow mind will notice is the bulk of the luggage carried by the passengers.

Indian families, travelling home to Calcutta, African families travelling home to Conackry, Addis Ababa, Khartoum, Ibadan – all with hordes of cousins, brothers, nephews, the lot . . . Students returning home after years of study on scholarships that were unnecessarily and intentionally extended, renewed and prolonged just because they wrote a letter to a cousin bureaucrat in the government back home expressing their desire to delay their return home. Government officials returning from study tours, whatever that means. On arrival they will tell reporters at the airport, "The tour was very successful," instead of saying, "I was very successful, I did a lot of shopping." Deported people shamefully returning to the motherlands they had shamelessly disowned. All these people converge at terminus 3 to enjoy their last contact with the so called civilized world, only to find themselves in the kind of commotion that the children of Israel found themselves in, on the night they left the honeypots of Egypt in a hurry.

This magnitude of people travel with excess luggage after buying items that are not available in their own countries. They will not have a chance to buy such items again unless they come back to Europe or America and only a few of them do come back. They buy soap, panties, bras, perfumes, ladies stockings, shoes, suits – you name it. All are scarce or unavailable but, essential commodities in the countries they are returning to. Some take home these items to sell at exorbitant prices, on the black market. They could fetch even a hundred times more their market value, where these items are unavailable or scarce, and where dressing the western way even if it means wearing an underwear or the bra from the developed world, is a symbol of keeping with the times.

Some of the items are presents for cousins, nephews, brothers, sisters and friends. Because when one arrives from the developed world, relatives, friends old and new – and there will be many, all converge at your house to shake your hand. They all say one thing, "Give me a present from overseas." You have to give each a present for how else will they know that you were in Europe or America?

Travellers at terminus 3 therefore carry a lot of stuff, so

they have a lot of luggage. The luggage is usually encased in various types of external covering – West African multicoloured mats, dyed clothing, artistically decorated barks of trees and banana leaves that have been treated to look like medieval clothing. Others carry modern suit cases as big as sea chests. Added to this atmosphere, the passengers, many dressed in African or oriental flamboyant attire give the appearance of an African market on a busy day. This is terminus 3 at London's Heathrow Airport.

Travelling by air is convenient and fast but it can be a mind boggling exercise, except for V.I.P.'s or International businessmen travelling first class. They have no problem because everything is done for them, from checking of luggage at the airport of entry to retrieving it at the airport of exit. The beautiful air hostesses even fasten the seat belts for the first class passengers, while you in the economy class would be busy fiddling with the seat belt wondering which way it buckles and unbuckles.

At the airport you always rush even if you arrive six hours before your flight is due. You go through the ticket office, luggage office, immigration and vaccination office and finally you are told your flight will be boarding at gate number such and such, and yet you are very far from the plane. You still have to go miles and miles down corridors, up and down escalators and all the time watching for the number of the gate your plane will be at while wondering, "Did they say 26 or 28?" because it makes a difference. You board at 26 and you end up in New Delhi, you board at 28 and you end up in Entebbe.

Finally you arrive, breathless, at gate 28 just in time to get, not on the plane, but on the bus to take you to your plane. You finally arrive at your flight. You are so tired that even the "Welcome aboard" smile from the air hostess that should lift the spirits of anybody, even those of a manic depressive patient does not soothe you!

Despite all these problems I managed to find my way around terminus 3 and boarded flight no 051 British Airways to Nairobi and Johannesburg. I was allocated a seat by the window. I had hoped that looking outside the window would keep my mind off Betty but that did not happen.

A Swedish lady occupied the seat next to me. We got talking, but before the plane took off she had already fallen asleep, so I sat sadly waiting for take off. All the time I was thinking about Betty among the luggage.

The air hostess brought the ear phones. The Swedish lady woke up and took hers, plucked into her ears and went to sleep, this time with her head on my shoulder. I closed my eyes and imagined that the warm head on my shoulder was Betty's. I saw Betty with her stretched black hair, her large eyes, her narrow forehead and long neck sleeping with her head on my shoulder. I wanted to raise my left arm and embrace her, press her head against my shoulder, feel her warmth. But then I was aware that the head on my shoulder was not hers. I opened my eyes, got tissue paper and wiped tears from my eyes.

Later the hostess brought us dinner. I woke up the Swedish girl but she said she was not eating. I said I was not eating either and ordered for a beer.

The flight was comfortable, yet I could not sleep. I drank a second beer and closed my eyes to try to sleep, but I kept on thinking about Betty. I was also thinking of what awaited me in Uganda. I was thinking of how I would get through the airport. I imagined that a soldier might shoot me at the airport and later there would be an announcement on Radio Uganda, "A Black Israelite had arrived in Uganda to take over the Presidency. Soldiers of the Ugandan Army shot him when he landed at Entebbe Airport." In Uganda they could do anything to anybody and explain the death in any words they liked. I chose not to care. They could shoot at me in the airport, they could feed my remains to crocodiles in the Nile. It was OK. What was the use of living with painful thoughts. However, if they killed me I would not deliver Betty's body to her uncle so that she could be buried in her father's coffee and banana plantation. If they killed me at the airport they would throw my body and Betty's into the Nile. I did not want Betty to be thrown into the Nile like her parents. I wanted Betty to be buried properly and on her tombstone be written her name and the names of her parents like she had wished. I concluded that I must stay alive to accomplish the mission.

I was not falling asleep so I took a 5mg tablet of valium and, thank God, sleep came. For a while I forgot my troubles. But I did not sleep forever and, I did not wish to sleep forever because I had a duty to do: to bury Betty's body at her birth place. I woke up and when I looked out of the window the sky was crimson in the East. There were still a few stars in the sky, scattered here and there. After a little while the sun came up. Darkness and the stars disappeared all at once. It was a spectacular site watching the sun rising over Africa from a boeing British Airways flight. I wished Betty was with me to see this wonderful sight.

We finally entered Kenyan airspace. The pilot pointed out Mount Kenya to us. It lay to our left rising above the plains that stretched to the horizon.

"Ladies and gentlemen, we have landed at Nairobi's Jomo Kenyatta International Airport. Those proceeding to Johannesburg kindly stay on board. For those disembarking here, I would like to say that we have enjoyed flying you from London. Please do not forget to take your chloroquine tablets. You are now in a Malarial area. Again thank you and goodbye."

After this short speech on the intercom, I bid goodbye to the Swedish lady, who was continuing to Johannesburg, and left the plane.

Despite all my sorrows I was happy to return to Africa. As I came down the ladder marked Kenya Airways, I felt very elated looking at the Kenyan ground crew in the Kenya Airways uniform. The girls looked so beautiful. I realised that one has to be away from Africa for a while to realise how beautiful African women are.

Disembarking from an airplane in developing countries is more entertaining than disembarking at Frankfurt, London, New York, Boston or any of those airports where you walk from the place right into carpeted corridors and lounges. The policemen, the security people and the fast walking serious crowds create an atmosphere very different from the atmosphere at Nairobi or Dar es Salaam airport. At Nairobi or Dar es Salaam you walk down the ladder into the warm tropical atmosphere, while being watched by the crowd on the balcony. You come down the ladder smiling and unwinding from the serious tense atmosphere in the plane, then you immediately set your foot on the African soil and walk to the immigration building. Of course, it is uncomfortable if you happen to land when there is a tropical downpour but on an ordinary day you enjoy coming down the ladder from the plane and stepping right on the African soil.

I was to continue to Entebbe by Kenya Airways. At the transit desk I was informed by a beautiful Kenya Airways attendant that my flight would leave in two hours time. She looked at my ticket and the attached luggage tags and knew that I was accompanying a dead body. I could see that she felt sorry for me.

"Is it your relative?"

"Yes," I said, "How is the situation in Uganda?"

She looked at me and said, "Fine, I guess."

I felt very lonely at the airport. I was approaching Uganda, the land of troubles, to lay Betty to rest and I needed all the courage and strength. I had not had a meal for a long time. I wanted to go and take breakfast at the airport cafeteria but before I could do that, an idea got into my mind, "Why not go to one of the windows and watch as they transfer Betty's coffin from the British Airways plane to the Kenya Airways one?" I had not seen the coffin since I had first seen it at the funeral home in Boston. I hoped that the roses I wanted fixed on top of the coffin were still there. I went to a nearby window and watched. People were busy attending to planes but there was no sight of a coffin so I decided to go to the cafeteria, although I knew my appetite was not good.

Despite lack of appetite I ate more food than I had ever eaten since Betty died. I think my appetite improved because the atmosphere in the cafeteria was so good. The waiters, many of them in their fifties, well dressed in white; were polite and joyful. They talked among themselves and with the customers in Kiswahili, a language I had not heard since I left Dar es Salaam. One of them on learning that I was from Tanzania, became so friendly and offered to get me some more fried eggs after seeing how fast I had finished the two that he had brought me. I declined but accepted a third glass of milk. The fresh milk tasted so much better than the milk I used to buy from the supermarket in Boston.

Chapter 11

Uganda

The Kenya Airways flight from Nairobi to Entebbe was only half full in contrast to the crowded British Airways flight from London to Johannesburg. What with the murderous regime! Very few people were travelling to Uganda.

I sat all alone by the window. I was deep in thought thinking of what lay ahead.

I was at the same time thinking about Betty's relatives. I was sure that they were now waiting for "us" at the airport. I hoped that the secret message that Betty's brother said he would send to his uncle in Uganda had already arrived. I hoped they did as Betty's brother had said. That is, send only two or three people to the airport in order to avoid being harassed by the army. I hoped there would not be too much waiting at the airport. I was sure there would be a lot of tears. It would definitely be very hard for them to see Betty, the small high school girl who had left Uganda smiling and happy, now being brought home in a coffin. I was imagining the turmoil, the cries of women and the shaking of heads in disbelief on arriving with the body in the village.

My thoughts were broken with, "Ladies and gentlemen, we shall soon land at Entebbe Airport, please fasten your seat belts and prepare for landing." I looked out of the window. We were flying over the blue waters of Lake Victoria. A ship probably the *MV Usoga* was sailing towards the clearly visible town of Jinja. I saw the source of the River Nile. In the past when pilots were entering Uganda, they would point out to the passengers, the source of the Nile and even the town of Jinja when they flew above them, but now they did not bother. It seemed that they, just as the passengers, were not happy to fly into Uganda. They were also pre-occupied with the eminent danger that lay ahead of them and so they did not bother to point out to the passengers important landmarks. Below us, I could see the Entebbe Road winding its way into Kampala. It used to be a beautiful road, but now one could see even from the air the many pot holes made on the tarmac by army tanks, as they escorted Idi Amin to and from the airport on his many out of the country trips to buy arms. The little traffic that was now on the road raised clouds of dust as if it was a drive down a village road.

We were now flying over land dotted with houses surrounded by thick banana and coffee trees. Ahead of us was the airport building. As we approached the runway, I saw on my left several MIG – 11's. They must have been about twenty. They were parked, sitting there as if preparing for an imminent Third World War. We finally landed and taxied to the airport building. The voice on the intercom simply said, "We have landed at Entebbe Airport." The air hostess did not bother to go into, "We are happy to have travelled with you. We hope to see you again on board soon. Have a pleasant stay in Uganda." After all, members of the crew were not happy to fly into Uganda. They did not bother to wish us a pleasant stay because they knew that it was impossible to have a pleasant stay in Uganda. They did not say that they hoped to fly with us again soon, because who knew if we would survive the stay in Uganda, where killings and disappearances were the order of the day!

The air hostess at the door was in a very good mood though. I guessed she was not bothered as long as she was not going to step on Ugandan soil, because the plane was to take off for Nairobi in half an hour's time. She gave us an encouraging smile and said, "Goodbye," to each of us as we walked down the ramp to step on Ugandan soil.

On the waving bay, above us, one could see soldiers with machine guns. The soldiers were watching us. In fact we felt as if we were prisoners of war because we felt as if we were walking right into the hands of the Ugandan Army. All, but a few, of the ground crew were soldiers in uniform. They regarded each of us with suspicion as they directed us to the immigration desk.

Disembarking at Entebbe Airport was certainly different from what it used to be in Dar es Salaam when returning from one of my overseas trips. At Dar es Salam, I would be greeted by Miriam, my secretary, "Did you have a nice trip?" "Yes thank you, how is Chief? I would answer. The driver would throw my bags in the boot of the Mercedes Benz and we would head for my house, where Miriam and I would eat some barbecued goat ribs, washed down by expensive wines I had picked up at some international airport abroad. Miriam always informed my cook, Juma, of my coming and he knew that there was nothing I liked and always missed during my trip abroad as barbecued goat ribs.

Being back home it would all be work again. During the drive from the airport to my house at Msasani Peninsula and while eating at the house and during the drive to the office, Miriam would brief me on the problems that I would immediately handle. From the house, I would go straight to the office, sit at my huge mahogany desk and start on work that had accumulated during my absence.

Today, at Entebbe Airport, there was no Miriam and there was no black Mercedes waiting for me.

At the immigration desk the clerk examined my passport for what looked like a century. He opened and read each page of the passport about four times. All this time a soldier in combat uniform stood by my side. At one time I thought, "Why doesn't he merely take the pistol from his hip and shoot me." I was fed up with all the unfairness in the world. Here was I, an innocent African returning to Africa to bury an African sister, and being kept waiting for a century with a soldier standing by my side as if I was a prisoner of war!

Finally the clerk told the soldier something in what sounded like Lugbara to me. The soldier beckoned me to an inner office where I found a fierce looking middle aged man in a rocking chair. He asked me a lot of questions which I answered, by the look on his face, satisfactorily. I had to explain what had brought me to Uganda, how long I was going to stay and where I was going to stay. My papers, or rather the papers from the hospital with the death certificate and post mortem report told the story. I was not a terrorist who had been sent in to kill the president. I had come in to bring the body of my girlfriend to be buried at her home.

The army officer was satisfied with my explanation about why I had come to Uganda. I am sure he did not realise that Betty was the daughter of a former minister in Obote's government, otherwise he would have ruled that my fate and the fate of Betty's body would have to be decided by a military tribunal.

I was now allowed to go and pick up my luggage. Two suitcases containing Betty's belongings and the coffin had been carelessly placed in one corner of the luggage chamber. The roses I had had the mortician place on the coffin were still there. They still looked fresh. It seemed that the coffin was handled all the way by civilized people. Now it had fallen into the hands of uncivilized people because as I went through customs, one of the soldiers accompanied me to look at the coffin. He told me to open it. He put his hands in it and manhandled Betty's body. He touched and pressed her from head to toe. I shuddered. In real life he would not have laid his dirty hands on her. He placed his hands in all corners of the coffin. He was looking for hidden guns no doubt. He did not find any, of course. The sight of this uncivilized man manhandling Betty's body like that was disgusting and humiliating. All that I could do was to look away and wipe the tears in my eyes. I could have killed the soldier if I had my way.

Nevertheless, I had to hold myself together because I was sure Betty's relatives were waiting for me. I was not to break down when they wanted me to stand by them during this sad moment.

One of the soldiers at the airport upon seeing my agony came to me and said, "Take it easy, brother, we have to check every luggage even if it is a coffin."

He then stayed by my side from there on till I left the airport with the coffin and Betty's relatives. He tried to help. He even helped us put the coffin in the pickup that was waiting to take the coffin to the village.

After I was allowed to go outside the airport building, I walked unsteadily to meet Betty's relatives. I recognized them immediately. Three sad looking gentlemen standing in the in-coming passengers lounge. I immediately fell in their arms. In fact I think I collapsed in their arms. For a minute or so I was not aware of myself as I hugged and embraced them. Later we greeted each other.

I managed to say through tight lips, "It is the wish of the Lord, not ours, so let's thank him for whatever he has given us and ask him to keep us strong during this hour of mourning."

I was not a very religious person but during my life I had always found a few religious words very soothing during times of agony.

We felt that we had to leave the airport immediately and, without wasting time on introductions, we put the coffin into the pickup and left.

We left the airport and found ourselves driving down Entebbe Road into the city of Kampala. I noticed that the road had really changed from the beautiful smooth road I saw six years back before the coup, when I had accompanied the Minister for Finance here on an official visit, to what looked almost like a village road.

The beautiful pavements had turned into rough side-

130

walks and the cool breeze that one could feel when driving down the road had turned into a dusty wind. There were emaciated dogs, sheep and goats roaming everywhere. Hand carts were many because as I guessed, the cost of petrol left no choice for many people except to use hand carts driven by human power. Traffic was dense and slow due to the numerous pot-holes on the road and the driver had to cleverly dodge them. He seemed used to doing this sort of thing.

He dodged a taxi, an ambulance and a fire truck which, I thought, he was going to run into all at once. A lorry carrying sand sped out of nowhere right into the road in front of us at high speed and created a monsoon of sand that blinded the driver. The driver cursed and called the driver of the lorry something that sounded to me like son of a bitch. The driver of the lorry disappeared into the thick traffic cleverly dodging carts, dogs, sheep, goats and fellow motorists.

A goat crossed the road and was followed by twin baby goats, the driver dodged the twin goats and almost ran into a hand cart carrying matoke.

Then we drove over a dead dog. I could smell it; it had been dead on the road for days!

As we were driving through Najja Nankumbi we saw six dead bodies on the roadside. They had been shot by soldiers the previous night and they were still lying there for people to see and know what could happen to them if they "misbehaved."

We left Entebbe Road into Nakivubo Road and entered Kampala. As we drove through the bus station we saw a mob administering instant "justice" to their fellow Ugandan. The man was lying on the ground bleeding from the nose and a head wound while the mob was throwing stones and bottles at him. I was sure they were going to crack his skull. I looked the other side of the road before the stone hit the man's skull, but still in my mind I could feel the impact and I could see his brain matter and blood flying everywhere.

We drove through Kampala, I noticed that shops were either closed or open but empty of goods. We entered Ndebba Road then Masaka Road and finally we were on our way to Mpigi.

We did not talk much on the way. Betty's uncle was a quiet, heart-broken man. I later learnt that he had been reduced from a very rich man to a pauper after soldiers had broken into his shop, stolen everything and burnt down the building. His son had been killed and his sixteen year old daughter was pregnant after a soldier raped her.

We arrived at Betty's home to find a crowd waiting for us. Women threw themselves down in agony. The cries were saddening. Everybody, even men, cried as the body was taken from the pickup truck and transferred to the house, a brickhouse that had bullet marks all over the walls.

It was a night of mourning. Hundreds of men and women came to the house, where we sat outside in the dim light of a kerosene lamp, while Betty's body lay in the coffin inside the house. The conversation among the mourners was in Luganda, but I could follow some of the things they were saying. There was fear among them that soldiers might come to kill them. They took every opportunity to engage in mass killings, especially at market places, during worship or even during funerals.

Fortunately no soldiers came in that night. In the morning we took Betty's body to church. Father Mcmahon said a requiem mass for Betty, blessed her body and we proceeded back to the homestead to bury her beside her grandfather's grave. I had shed tears throughout the requiem mass and, I thought I had no more tears left, but at the graveside I cried openly. I noticed that they had left space for two graves between Betty's grandfather's grave and hers to mark the graves for Betty's parents. I had remembered to tell Betty's uncle that Betty had wished the names of her parents to be written on her epitaph to say, "Here lie three of us . . ."

After the burial Betty's uncle closed the ceremony at the graveside with:

"Aboluganda, Abako n'abemikwano. Nyimilidde wano okubebeza olwo 'kujja okuziika omwana waffe Betty eyafira mu Amerika. Nebaza mikwano gyomugenzi gyamugenzi gyabadde, abamujanjaba nga mulwadde era abayambye okusobozesa okuleeta omulambo okugutusa mu Uganda. Nokusingira ddala omwami awerekedde omulambo era goe tuli naye wano. Omwana ono ye Betty yazalibwa mu 1959, Yasomera Nakasero Primary School, Oluvunyuma nagenda Gayaza High School. Geyamalila Senior Six. Yagenda mu Amerika St. Francis College Boston okusomera B.A

Betty yafe Lubya mira.

Bonange muwaddeyo amagubo ga Shs. 80,000 na embugo enkalu. Aboluganda mwenna mbebazizza nnyo olwebyo byemukoze mukama abayambe nga muddayo buli omu mu mkage."

My Brothers, Clansmen and Friends, I stand here to thank you for coming to bury our child Betty who died in America. I thank friends of the late Betty who nursed her when she was sick and who helped bring her body to Uganda, especially this gentleman we are with here today who escorted the body back home to Uganda.

Our child Betty was born in 1959. She went
to Nakasero Primary School, then to Gayaza
High School where she completed Senior Six.
From there she went to St. Francis College
in Boston U.S.A. She died of pneumonia.

Friends, you have contributed eighty
thousand shillings. There are also many
other things that you have contributed. I
thank you all very much for all that you
have done. May the Almighty watch over all
of you on your way home.

I stayed with Betty's people for one week, spending most
of the time sitting on a stool or on a mat on the verandah,
talking to the people who came to mourn. Fortunately, in
Uganda many people speak English. I recounted on and on
to the mourners how Betty had died. Sometimes a young
man would translate to the old people in Luganda and when
he finished they would all say, *"Ngolabie."*

The cries of women would often bring tears to my eyes,
though no other man was crying. The men sat sadly on mats.
They would often shake their heads in disbelief and often
say, *"Kitalonyo."*

Sometimes, I would just wonder around in the coffee
plantations thinking of Betty. I was on one of my afternoon
rounds in the banana and coffee plantations when I saw
them – three soldiers watching the crowd that gathered in
the homestead. They were tall, their heads rising high above
the coffee trees. They were almost as tall as the banana trees.
The muzzles of their guns were barely visible above the
coffee trees. The colour of their combat uniform merged
with the green of the banana and coffee trees. I thought that
they were Acholis, but I was not sure.

I retreated slowly to the house and with a trembling voice I whispered to Betty's uncle, "Look, there are soldiers out there."

He looked at me as if it did not matter and said, "We are used to seeing them. There is nothing we can do if they want to kill us. They have been killing our people ever since the coup in 1971."

They did not come to kill us, though. They came to the home and demanded for beer, drank lots of it and left without a word of sympathy. They did not greet anyone. As far as they were concerned, they had walked into a beer party. They drank, were satisfied and left after they had been assured that we had gathered to mourn and not to plan to topple the government.

As it usually happens, the shaving of heads ceremony took place on the third day after the burial. Betty's uncle insisted on shaving his head completely clean. He said, "When my brother died I did not dare shave my head for fear of being killed, too, so now, I'll shave to mourn my brother and niece at the same time."

As for the other relatives, the shaving ceremony was simplified. The neighbour who was conducting the shaving ceremony simply cut a few hairs from the centre of each person's head. I also took part in the shaving ceremony. A bit of hair was cut from the centre of my head and when this was being done somebody asked, "Who is that? Is he one of Betty's relatives?"

Somebody answered in Luganda, *"Omusajja wa Betty."*

Seven days after the burial, I had to leave for Boston. I wished I could wait for the *olumbe* ceremony, but I had to go back to school in U.S.A. Betty had said, "Do not let my death send you into a mental hospital. You must go on studying and go back home to become a principal secretary."

On my return to Boston I wrote away my sorrows and loneliness through the cold winter. Winter was so severe that I feared that I might catch pneumonia and die like Betty had done , but I survived. When the first flowers of spring began to appear, I was still writing this manuscript and thinking about her all the time. I would sometimes see in my mind the flowering plants we had planted on the mound of soil under which she lay.

Summer is here. Everybody is exploding with the joy of summer. The exams are approaching. I am spending lots of time reading and worrying about the exams but, I know I shall pass and graduate with a Master's Degree in Economics and return home. Chief will be very happy when he sees me back with my Master's Degree in Economics. He had predicted right that I might meet my future wife in U.S.A. Yes, I did meet her, but I never got to make her my wife. Death took her from me before I got married to her. Chief had said that people go to study overseas and they return with two certificates; one academic and the other marital. If it were not for the fatal pneumonia that took Betty's life, I too would have returned with both.

In Boston, summer can sometimes be unbearably hot. I am now sweating in my hot and dry studio apartment. I miss my air conditioned office in Dar es Salaam and my cool Msasani Peninsula home, but most of all I miss Betty. As I finish this story, this day in Boston, I feel sad instead of being happy. All the time I have been writing, I felt very close to her, but now as I write these last lines, I feel as if I am parting with her afresh. I feel just like I felt on that day I saw her buried in Uganda, on the coffee and banana plantation that belonged to her father. But I will not forget her, even though I have finished writing this story. I will now lay down my pen and lie in bed in this hot, lonely apartment in Boston, and dream of my Betty who is lying under the tropical flowers in a grave in Uganda. I will also dream of this manuscript about her.

The End